CAGED

CAGED

Memories Have Names

GULZAR

Translated by SATHYA SARAN

PENGUIN

An imprint of Penguin Random House

HAMISH HAMILTON

Hamish Hamilton is an imprint of the Penguin Random House group of companies whose addresses can be found at global.penguinrandomhouse.com

Published by Penguin Random House India Pvt. Ltd
4th Floor, Capital Tower 1, MG Road,
Gurugram 122 002, Haryana, India

Penguin
Random House
India

First published in Hamish Hamilton by Penguin Random House India 2024

ISBN 9780670098231

Typeset in Mrs Eaves OT by Manipal Technologies Limited, Manipal
Printed at Thomson Press India Ltd, New Delhi

www.penguin.co.in

Abbu ke Naam . . .

Contents

II

III

IV

Caged . . .

I was trying to catch a butterfly. She escaped, but left her colours on my fingers.

That's what happens with some colourful moments too; they tint the memory with unforgettable images.

These poems are the imprints of some faces and personalities that presented themselves to me, when I tried to preserve them in memory.

Most of them are of well-known people. Some are great legends too. Legends like Birju Maharaj, Salil Chowdhury, Mehdi Hasan, Jatin Das, Pancham, Naam Dev, Asha Bhosle. I painted their portraits with images in words.

Then there are some people who showered very colourful moments on my life. They keep fluttering around me: Meghna, Raakhee, Vishal, Naseer, Javed Sahab, to name a few.

Some are unknown to people. But I will name them, and the poems will introduce them to you.

Gulzar

Translator's Note

He was trying to catch a butterfly. I was trying to catch a poet. Through his poems.

The butterfly left its colours on his fingers; I got, instead, images and glimpses. Sometimes of the poet, sometimes of the kaleidoscope of colours he was transferring on to paper. They flitted through the words, shifting images that left strangely definite impressions on the mind.

Now the book is done, and I have wandered through the words, and sifted the images, trying to trap them in pages of a different voice. Their stories remain with me. Of painters, writers and singers, of people known of and admired. Among them, Salil Chowdhury, Asha Bhosle, Naseeruddin Shah, Rabindranath Tagore, Van Gogh . . . Many others whom I had not known before . . . Gopichand Narang, Jibanananda Das, Sukhbir . . . I have met them all now and taken their measure. And their stories remain.

The others, unknown, sometimes nameless; their stories too I heard; colours spilling from the poet's pen.

A translator's task demands matching steps on a little-known path with someone who has laid the path, knows the route and is aware of where it leads. A path that a poet like Gulzar lays out studded with surprises. Surprises that ease the frown from the brow and draw a smile at the curve of the mouth, surprises that need to be caught and trapped into a new idiom.

Translating Hindustani into English, as anyone who has attempted this knows, shows up the huge emotional and cultural differences between the two languages. Brevity that works so well in one, struggles for expression in the other. The rhythms of speech differ. But translators soldier on. And I have tried to keep the flavour and mood of the original as far as the language allows.

It's been a journey, this slender volume of translated work; a journey through a changing light where words and images played together in the original to capture the men and women Gulzar admires, loves, lived or worked with; or someone he met on a flight or through the ringing of the phone at night, people who remain with him. You, reader will meet them too.

And like they did with me, they will stop to tell you their stories. As only Gulzar can tell them.

Sathya Saran

I

राबिंद्रनाथ टैगोर

पूरे बँगाल में फ़सल की तरह उगा हुआ एक शायर। पूरे इलाक़े पर मुसलसल बरसता हुआ आसमान। हर घर में पौधे की तरह लगा हुआ है। सिर्फ़ एक शायर नहीं, एक अकेला शख़्स पूरे बँगाल का कलचर है। बहुत छुटपन ही में उनकी शायरी छू गयी थी। उन्हीं को पढ़ने के लिये बड़े हो कर बँगला सीखी—और 'बँगला' सीखते सीखते ज़िंदगी का रुख़ ही बदल गया . . . ब्याहे गये बँगला से।

राबिंद्रनाथ टैगोर: पोट्रेट

गाँव से लगी हुई नदी है,
जिसपे बारह मास बूँद बूँद आसमाँ बरसता है
जलतरंग बजता है
'जोल पोड़े, पाता नोड़े . . . पाता नोड़े, जोल पोड़े'

सारा गाँव जलतरँग के बोल
कियारियों में बो के सींचा करते हैं
बीज फूटते हैं तो,
कोंपलें निकलती हैं, पर लगे ख़्यालों की

Rabindranath Tagore

A poet who stands like a crop, growing across all of Bengal. A sky sending constant rain that falls gently on every locality and district. Growing like a plant in every home. Not just a poet, but the cartographer of the entire state's culture.

I was touched by his poetry while still very young. Just so I could read him, I learnt Bangla. And even as I studied Bangla, it changed the face of my life.

I wedded Bangla.

Rabindranath Tagore: A Portrait

A river flows alongside the village
Over which through the months of the year
The sky sends unending drops of rain
And the Jal Tarang sings out
'Jol pode, pata node, pata node, jol pode'
The rain falls, the leaves flutter.

The entire village
Sows the words of the Jal Tarang
In rows and rows of earth beds.
When the seeds burst open,
Buds peer out,

लफ़्ज़ जब पलक पलक उठा के देखते हैं तो
नज़्म आँख खोलती है शाख़ पर

इक फ़सल की तरह
उगा हुआ ज़मीन पर
एक शख़्स
आस पास बारह मास गुनगुनाता है
'जोल पोड़े, पाता नोड़े . . .
पाता नोड़े, जोल पोड़े'

गाँव से लगी हुई नदी है, इक भरी हुई
जिसपे बारह मास बूँद बूँद आसमाँ बरसता है!

Like rows of words, one by one,
Poems start to blink wide-eyed on the branches.

Standing like a crop, someone on a high slope,
Through the months of the year,
Hums a song
'Jol pode, pata node, pata node, jol pode'
The rain falls, the leaves flutter, the leaves flutter, the rain falls.

The village has a river running alongside it, brim to brim
On which the sky drops its rain, through the year.

टैगोर

एक देहाती सर पे गुड़ की भेली बाँधे
लम्बे चौड़े इक मैदाँ से गुज़र रहा था
गुड़ की ख़ुशबू सुनके भिन भिन करती
इक छत्ती सर पे मँडलाती थी
धूप चढ़ती और सूरज की गर्मी पहुँची तो
गुड़ की भेली बहने लगी

मासूम देहाती हैराँ था
माथे से मीठे मीठे क़तरे गिरते थे
और वो जीभ से चाट रहा था!

मैं देहाती . . .
मेरे सर पर ये टैगोर की कविता की भेली किसने रख दी!

Tagore

With a chunk of gur tied on his head, a rustic
Was crossing a vast maidan, both long and wide
Hearing the fragrance of the gur,
A canopy of bees hummed over his head
The sun rose higher and in the growing heat
The gur started to melt.

The simple villager was now astonished,
Drops of gur were running down his face
And he was licking them with his tongue.

I'm a simple villager,
Who has placed the sweet gur of Tagore's poems
On my head?

ग़ालिब

होगा कोई ऐसा भी, कि ग़ालिब को न जाने
शायर तो वो अच्छा है, पर बदनाम बहुत है!

ग़ालिब ख़ुद अपना तारुफ़ इसी तरह कराते हैं। ऐसी शोख़ी किसी और शायर में देखी और न सुनी . . . और बला की ख़ुद्दारी।

बाज़ीचा-ए-अतफ़ाल है, दुनिया मेरे आगे
होता है शब-व-रोज़, तमाशा मेरे आगे

यक़ीन मानिये, मैंने हिंदुस्तान की हर ज़बान की शायरी पढ़ी है, और सुनी है ओरीजनल और तर्जुमों में भी। लेकिन इस मिज़ाज का शायर, उर्दू के इलावा किसी ज़बान में नहीं पाया। ग़ालिब उर्दू ज़बान का एक और नाम है। और बे-नाम-व-निशाँ होने की ये ख़्वाहिश सुनिये!

Ghalib

'Is there a man who does not know of Ghalib
A good poet he surely is, but infamous . . . '

Ghalib describes himself thus.

Such mischief is not seen or heard in any other poet. And then there was his devilish ego!

'Bazeecha-e-atphal hai duniya mere aagey
Hota hai shab-va-roz tamasha mere aagey'

The world, a child's playground, it seems to me
Endlessly, the play of life is enacted before me.

Please believe me when I say I have read the poets of India in every language; both in the original and in translation. But I have not found a poet of this temperament in any language besides Urdu. Ghalib is a synonym for the Urdu language.

Now listen to his desire to vanish without a trace:

हुए मर के हम जो रुसवा, हुए क्यों न ग़र्क़े दरया
न कहीं जनाज़ा उठता, न कहीं मज़ार होता

और मैं उन्हें बल्लीमाराँ के मोहल्ले में तलाश कर रहा था।

ग़ालिब: पोटेरेट

बल्लीमाराँ के मोहल्लों की वो पेचीदा दलीलों की सी गलियाँ
सामने टाल के नुक्कड़ पे, बटेरों के क़सीदे
गुड़गुड़ाती हुई पान की पीकों में वो दाद, वाह वा . . .
चंद दरवाज़ों पे लटके हुए बोसीदा से कुछ टाट के पर्दे
एक बकरी के मिमयाने की आवाज़
और धुँधलायी हुई शाम के बेनूर अँधेरे साये

ऐसे दीवारों से मुँह जोड़ के चलते हैं यहाँ
'चूड़ीवालान' के कटरे की 'बड़ी बी' जैसे
अपनी बुझती हुई आँखों से दरवाज़े टटोले
इसी बेनूर अँधेरी सी 'गली क़ासिम' से
एक तरतीब चिराग़ों की शुरू होती है
एक कुरान-ए-सुख़न का सफ़्हा खुलता है
'असद उल्लाह ख़ाँ ग़ालिब' का पता मिलता है!

'Huey mar ke jo hum ruswa, Huey kyon na garke dariya
Na kahin janaza uthta, Na kahin mazaar hota'

Dishonoured I was after my death.
Why did I not drown myself
There would have been no funeral then
Nor a tomb built for me anywhere.

And I was searching for him in the lanes of Ballimaran!

Ghalib: A Portrait

The lanes of Ballimaran that like 'tedious arguments' run*
Discussing partridges at the street corner
The gurgle of praise by people with mouths full of paan
Curtains of tattered jute hang from some doorways
The sound of a goat bleating
And the gloomy shadows of the evening mists

Move so closely embracing the walls as if
Badi bi of Chudiwalan, with dimmed sight,
Is groping her way to find the door.
From this gloomy and dark *gali quasim*
Lamps send out trails of light
A page opens in the Koran of the intellect
And the address of Assadullah Khan Ghalib's home is revealed!

----
* T. S. Eliott

ग़ालिब—म्यूज़ियम गली क़ासिम

गली क़ासिम में आकर
तुम्हारी डेवढ़ी पर रुक गया हूँ, मिर्ज़ा नौशा !
तुम्हें आवाज़ दूँ पहले . . .
चली जायें ज़रा पर्दे में उमराव
तो फिर अंदर क़दम रक्खूँ

चिलमची, लोटा, सीनी, उठ गये हैं
बरसता था जो दो घँटे को मीन्हा,
छत चार घँटे तक बरसती थी . . .
उसी छलनी सी छत की अब मर्म्मत हो रही है
सदी से कुछ ज़्यादा वक़्त आने में लगा,
अफ़सोस है मुझको !
असल में घर के बाहर कोयेलों के टाल की
सियाही लगी थी, वो मिटानी थी . . . उसी में बस
कई सरकारें बदली हैं तुम्हारे घर पहुँचने में !

जहाँ कल्लन को लेकर बैठते थे, याद है? बालाई मँज़िल पर ?
लिफ़ाफ़े जोड़ते थे तुम लई से
ख़तों की कश्तियों में उर्दू बहती थी
अछूते साहिल उर्दू नसर छूने लग गयी थी
वहीं बैठेगा कंप्यूटर . . .
वहाँ से लाखों ख़त भेजा करेगा

तुम्हारे दस्तख़त जैसे, वो ख़ुशख़त तो नहीं होंगे, मगर फिर भी . . .
पर्सतारों की गिन्ती भी असद, अब तो करोड़ों है

Ghalib—Museum Galli Quasim

Entering Galli Quasim
I have stopped at your mansion, Mirza Nausha
Let me call out to you,
First let Umrau go behind the curtains into purdah
Before I step inside.

Cooking vessels, the jug and tray are all removed
The rain used to fall for two hours
The roof would rain for four.
The same sieve-like roof is now being repaired . . .
That it took more than a hundred years for this,
Saddens me.
In fact, the smudges of the coal dump in your house had to be erased,
And meanwhile,
Many governments changed, before your house could be reached.

Where you would sit with Kallan on the upper floor, do you
        remember?
You would paste the sides of envelopes with gum,
On the boats of your letters Urdu would flow,
Flawless Urdu prose started lapping at untrodden shores . . .

Now a computer will take over the space.
A million letters will be dispatched from there.
They will not be as beautiful as those in your handwriting,

तुम्हारे हाथ के लिक्खे सफ़्हात रक्खे जा रहे हैं
तुम्हें तो याद होगा . . .
'मस्वदा' जब रामपूर से, लखनऊ से, आगरा तक घूमा करता था!

शिकायत थी तुम्हें,
'यारब न वो समझे हैं, न समझेंगे मेरी बात
दे और दिल उनको, जो न दे मुझको ज़बाँ और'

ज़माना हर ज़बाँ में पढ़ रहा है अब, तुम्हारे सब सुख़न ग़ालिब
समझते कितने है, ये तो वही समझें, या तुम समझो!

यहीं शीशों में लगवाये गये हैं पैरहन अब कुछ तुम्हारे
ज़रा सोचो तो क़िस्मत चार-गरह कपड़े की अब 'ग़ालिब'
कि थी क़िस्मत ये उस कपड़े की, 'ग़ालिब' का ग्रेबाँ था!

तुम्हारी टोपी रखी है . . .
जो अपने दौर से उँची पहनते थे
तुम्हारे जूते रक्खे हैं . . .
जिन्हें तुम हाथ में लेकर निकलते थे,
शिकायत थी कि सारे घर को ही, मस्जिद बना रखा है बेगम ने!

तुम्हारा बुत भी अब लगवा दिया है, ऊँचा क़द देकर,
जहाँ से देखते हो अब, तो सब बाज़िचाये अतफ़ाल लगता है!
सब कुछ है मगर नौशा . . .
अगरचा जानता हूँ, हाथ में जुँबिश नहीं बुत के
तुम्हारे सामने इक साग़र-व-मीना तो रख देते

But yet
Worshippers too, Asad, now number in millions
Pages written in your hand are being preserved here
You must surely remember
Manuscripts would from Rampur, to Lucknow, to Agra travel

You would complain,
'Oh God, they have not understood, nor will they understand me
Give them a kinder heart if you won't give me a different language.'

The world is reading your writing in every language, Ghalib
What sense they make of it, only they can understand. Or you can
       understand perhaps
Your clothes too have been placed here, in showcases
Just think of the luck of these tattered clothes now, Ghalib,
Which had the fortune to clothe Ghalib.

Your cap is kept there too,
Which you wore higher than was customary,
And your shoes too are kept,
Which you would hold in your hands as you left,
Complaining that your begum had turned the entire house into
       a masjid.

They've made a statue too of you, placed it on a pedestal
When you look down from it, everything must seem a child's play.
There's everything there, Nausha,
Yet I know
That the hand of the statue cannot move
But they should have placed a goblet of wine before you.

बस इक आवाज़ जो गूँजती रहती है अब घर में
न था कुछ तो ख़ुदा था, कुछ न होता तो ख़ुदा होता
डुबोया मुझको होने ने, न होता मैं तो क्या होता!

There's a voice that echoes through the house now
Na tha kuch toh khuda tha, na hota kuch toh khuda hota
Dubaya mujh ko hone ne, na hota main to kya hota.

'When there was nothing, there was God, if there was nothing, God
would still be there.
My existence has ruined me, if I did not exist, what would I be?'

जलालुद्दीन रूमी

रूमी मेरे लिये, लेजर पर बनी एक ईमेज है। जितना नज़र आता है, उतना नहीं है। उसके पीछे पूरी एक कायेनात नज़र आती है। कभी लगता है वो था ही नहीं। वो एक ख़्याल था जिसे वक़्त ने वजूद दे देया। या कोई इश्क़ था, जिसे वजूद मिल गया।

सूफ़ी दे सुलफ़े की
लौ उठके कहती है
आतिश ये बुझके भी
जलती ही रहती है!

जलालुद्दीन रूमी

पिछली एक पीढ़ी से
ऊँची एक सीढ़ी से
जाने क्या सुनाता है
पिलपिला सा बूढ़ा है
पीठ पर पड़ा हुआ
इक घना सा जुड़ा है
रातों को लपेट के
रखता है समेट के
कुछ ज़मीं से छानता है
कहता है वो जानता है

Jalaluddin Rumi

Rumi, to me, is an image made on a laser. Whatever is seen of him, as much remains invisible. Behind which an entire universe is visible. At times it feels as if he never existed. He was just a thought that time created. Or a love that acquired substance.

Rising from the smouldering coal
The flame of Sufi says
Even when it is extinguished
This fire continues to blaze.

Jalaluddin Rumi

Since a generation past
On a high ladder he stands steadfast

Who knows what he speaks of
The old man with body gone soft
Lying heavy on his back
Is a dense knot of hair
Wrapping up the night
He has folded it in tight.

मिट्टी ये फ़लक की है
कहकशा नमक की है

मिट्टी के सकोरों में
काँसी के कटोरों में
भरता ही तो रहता है
ढेर सारे बोरों में

चुटकी से उठाता है
हवाओं में उड़ाता है
जिसका जी करे चखे
जिसके जी लगे रखे

मिट्टी ये फ़लक की है
कहकशा नमक की है

कह रहा था कान में
कान झाड़ कर सुना
आँख से टपक गया
आबशार, गुनगुना

थोड़ा सा थका हुआ
थोड़ा सा झुका हुआ
इक सदी से वो वहीं
सीढ़ी पर रुका हुआ

He chooses things from the earth
Telling us that he knows
The soil has come from the universe
Carrying the salt of galaxies.

Earthen plates and cups
And bowls of *kaansa* made
And countless bags of jute
He keeps incessantly filling.

A pinch of it he takes
And throws into the air
Whoever wants, can taste it
Whoever cares, can take it.
The soil has come from the universe,
Carrying the salt of galaxies.

He was speaking in my ear,
Which I had dusted well to hear.
My eyes welled and dribbled
A cascade of water, tepid.

Somewhat tired was he
And a little bent
For a generation past
On the ladder he stands steadfast.

आसमाँ तले ज़मीं
कितनी बार घूमी है
वो हिला नहीं कभी
बूढ़ा क्या नजूमी है?

या वो तुर्की टोपी में
जलालुद्दीन रूमी है!

Under the sky, the earth
Has taken innumerable rounds,
He stands fast, unmoving yet
Is the old man a seer, a prophet?

Or he in the Turkish cap we see
Could he be Jalaluddin Rumi!

शेक्सपियर (1564–1616)

शेक्सपियर, किताबों के नये पुराने ऐडीशन के हिसाब से नये पुराने लगते हैं। पुराना ऐडीशन देखो तो सोल्हवी सदी के लगते हैं। नया ऐडीशन देखो तो लगता है फ़ोन करलें, वहीं होंगे Stratford में। नये नये adaptations देते रहते हैं! चार सौ साल बाद एक रोज़ (पर्दा उठने से पहले) wings में मिल गये।

शेक्सपियर

शेक्सपियर . . .
उठाओ पर्दा,
तुम्हारे किरदार मुन्तज़िर हैं
सभी ने पोशाकें भी पहन ली हैं अपनी अपनी
और मेकअप भी कर लिया है
मकालमे हिफ़्ज़ हैं सभी को
कि चार सौ साल बाद भी ज़िंदगी के
सारे तज़ाद (conflicts) अब भी उसी तरह हैं
अभी तलक कशमकश वहीं है,
To be or . . . not to be!

Shakespeare (1564–1616)

Depending on whether you are looking at old or new editions of his books, Shakespeare fits into both the old and the new. Check out an old edition, and he seems to belong to the sixteenth century. But look through a new edition and you feel, let's call him on the phone; he must still be there at Stratford.

He offers up new adaptations continuously. Four hundred years after his time, I finally met him in the wings, one day.

Shakespeare

Shakespeare . . .
Pull up the curtain
Your actors are waiting
All of them have donned their costumes
And applied their make-up too.
Everyone knows your lines by heart
That despite the passing of four hundred years
Life's conflicts remain the same,
The same indecision, the confusion . . .
To be . . . or not to be.

सभी को मालूम है दुनिया यह स्टेज है
एक और अदाकार हैं सभी हम
अभी तलक छुप के घर से, मासूम
'जुलियेट' झुक के बालकनी से
उसी तरह सर्गोशियाँ करतीं है अपने रोमियो से!
सियास्तों में उसी तरह मग़रूर Caesar
गिराये जाते हैं ख़ंजरों से
Et tu, Brute का जुमला सेनेट (senate) में गूँजता है

तुम्हारे किर्दार, 'ओथेलो', डेसडीमोना', 'मैकबैथ'
अभी तलक दिल दिमाग़ की उल्झनों से फ़ारिग़ नहीं हुए हैं

तीसरी घँटी बज चुकी है
Lights ऑन हो गयी है
तुम्हारे किर्दार मुन्तज़ि हैं, शेक्सपियर
उठाओ पर्दा . . . पर्दा उठाओ!

Everyone is aware that the world is a stage
And we are just actors.

Even now, quietly within her house
An innocent Juliet
Leaning from her balcony,
Continues to grapple with her Romeo

And vainglorious Caesars, proud
About their mode of governance
Are felled by unforgiving scimitars
Et tu Brute . . . the phrase
Echoes across the senate.

Your characters, Othello, Desdemona and Macbeth
Of turmoils of heart and mind are yet
To be freed.

The third bell has sounded,
The lights have come on
Your actors are a-waiting, Shakespeare,
Lift the curtain, pull it up.

अहमद नदीम क़ासमी

बाबा हैं मेरे . . .

    पाकिस्तान के अज़ीम अफ़साना निगार, शायर और सहाफ़ी। नब्बे बरस जिये और ज़िंदगी के आख़री दिन तक, आख़री कॉलम लिखा। 'फ़नून' रिसाला के एडीटर और मालिक! उर्दू में, मेरी पहली किताब पाकिस्तान में, बाबा ने छापी। जब भी पाकिस्तान जाऊँ, मैं पहला सजदा उनकी क़ब्र पर पेश करता हूँ। फिर मस्जिद में।

अहमद नदीम क़ासमी: पोर्ट्रेट

इक घना पेड़ है जिसकी घनी छाँव में
धूप उतरती है तो उतनी सी ज़मीं पर जैसे
सैंकड़ों लफ़्ज़ों के सिक्के से बिखर जाते हैं
गोल, चोकोर, चमकदार, तलाई सिक्के
जाने क्या लिखती है छाँव में पड़ी धूप वहाँ
मैं भी उस पेड़ की छाँव में गया हूँ बरसों
और भर लेता था इन सिक्कों से जेबें अपनी
और तन्हाई को पहलू में बिठा कर अक्सर
पहरों आहँग सुना करता था उन सिक्कों की!

Ahmad Nadeem Qasmi

I regard him as my elder, my Baba. Pakistan's greatest teller
of stories, poet and journalist. He lived to be ninety, and
continued to write till the very last day of his life. He owned and
edited that treasure-house of Urdu, 'Fanoon'. My first book in
Urdu printed in Pakistan was published by Baba. On any visit to
Pakistan, I bow my head first at his grave. Then at the masjid.

Ahmad Nadeem Qasmi: A Portrait

There stands a tree under whose thick shade
When the sun filters through
In that little space on the ground
It scatters words like coins
Thousands of which lie strewn around.
Round, square, shining, weighty coins.
Who knows what the sunlight writes
As she rests in the dappled shade.

I too have stood under this shade,
Many a time, over the years
And filled my pockets with these coins.
Then often with loneliness seated by my side
I have listened for hours to their music.

उनपे उभरे हुए चेहरों को पढ़ा करता था
कोई अफ़साना सुनाता था, कोई नज़्म कभी
अब भी जाता हूँ मैं जब अपने सख़ी पेड़ के पास
तो वो भर देता है झब से मेरी ख़ाली झोली
वो सख़ी पेड़ मेरा दोस्त, मेरा बाबा है!

I would read the faces that emerged
One would tell a story at times, another a *nazm*.
Even now when I visit the bounteous tree
He quickly fills up my empty bag
That bounteous tree is my friend, my baba.

बाबा . . .

जब चिराग़ बुझता है
इक धुआँ सा उठता है
आफ़ताब शाम को
जब ग़ुरूब होता है
टीन का फ़लक भी तो
देर तक सुलगता है
पत्ते टूटते हैं तो
थोड़ी दूर उड़ते हैं
तुमने जाते वक़्त क्यों
मुड़ के देखा भी नहीं
साँस रोकी और तुम
मिट्टी ओढ़ सो गये!

Baba . . .

When the lamp burns out
A slight smoke rises
When the diminished sun sets
Long after sunset
The sky of steel glows with its light
When leaves break away
They float for a distance.

Why then, while you were leaving
Did you not turn and look back even once?
Just held your breath and
Wrapped in soil, you went to sleep.

सुनीलदा

आप उन्हें सुनील गंगोपाध्याय के नाम से जानते हैं। मैं उनकी कहानियों से वाक़िफ़ था, फिर नज़्मों से वाक़्फ़ियत हुआ और उसके बाद नोवेलों से मिला। निहायत सुरीले, और मोहब्बतों से छलके हुए इंसान। मुझसे बड़े थे मगर मुझे कभी छोटा नहीं महसूस होने दिया। पढ़ते बहुत थे . . .

> 'किताब औंधी पड़ी है मेज़ पर
> रहने दो उसको!'

सुनीलदा

किताब औंधी पड़ी है मेज़ पर,
रहने दो उसको
उसे नींद आ गई थी पढ़ते पढ़ते
वो उठ कर सो गया था
अगरचा पौ फटे सूरज ने झाँका भी था,
दस्तक दी थी खिड़की पर
हवा ने आके सहलाया था उसको
मगर जागा नहीं, न उसने करवट ली!

Sunil Da

You know him as Sunil Gangopadhyay. I was familiar with his stories; then acquainted myself with his poems, and after that met with his novels. A very musically tuned soul, brimming with affection. Though he was the bigger person in every way, he never made me feel lesser than him. He read a lot . . .

> The book lies open face down, on the table
> Let it be . . .

Sunil Da

The book lies open, face down
Let it be so . . .
He fell asleep while reading.
He moved to the bed and went to sleep.
Though at daybreak, the sun did peep in,
It even knocked on his window
And the breeze entered to touch him with a caress,
He did not awaken; nor did he turn on his side.

बयाँ जारी है दोस्त उसका अदब में
किताब औंधी पड़ी है, रहने दो उसको
उठेगा तो . . .
उसी सफ़हे से आगे पढ़ना हो शायद!

His discourse continues in literature

The book lies open, face down

Let it remain so . . .

If he should wake, he may like to continue

From the same page, perhaps . . .

जीवनानन्द दास

अगर ख़ुदा, इंसान को अपने हाथों से घड़ता है तो जीवनानन्द दास को ख़ुदा ने किसी गहरे समंदर की तह से मिट्टी निकाल के बनाया होगा। उनकी इमेजरी किसी चील के परों से फिसलती धूप से चुनी गई है।

बड़ी तकलीफ़ होती है जान कर कि . . .
तारकोल की सड़क पर चलते हुए, ट्राम के नीचे आकर उनकी मौत हुई!

जीवनानन्द दास

मैं आधी नींद में था उसने जब आवाज़ दी थी
वो शायद कूद के उतरा था चलती ट्राम से और . . .
और झील के पानी में पाँव जा पड़ा था
झील के पानी से राजहँस अपने दोनों
पँख खोले, शायें शायें उड़ गया था
'शुनाली' धूप की महकार पँखों से गिरा के
चील अपने आशियाँ में लौट आई!

मैं आधी नींद में हूँ . . .
धुआँ है, झटपटा है शाम का, जाड़ों का कोहरा,
और उस में ट्राम की दो पट्रीयाँ हैं
पट्रीयों में ख़ूँ चमकता है

Jibanananda Das

If God indeed does shape men with his own hands, then he must have used the clay from the base of a deep sea to create Jibanananda Das.

His imagery was lifted from the sunshine sliding on the wings of a soaring eagle.

It gave me great pain to know that . . . while walking on the tarred city road, he lost his life under the wheels of a tram.

Jibanananda Das

I was half asleep when he called out.
Perhaps he had jumped down from a moving tram, and . . .
His feet splashed into the waters of a lake
Spreading both his wings the swan had left the lake
Had flown away with a 'shain shain' sound,
Shedding the 'shunali' fragrance from its wings
The eagle to its nest has returned.

I am half asleep
Smoke is in the air, the hurry burry of the evening,
and winter's mists
And the twin rails of the tram
Blood shines dully on the rails

कोई दो पट्टीयों के बीच पढ़ता आ रहा है नज़्म 'बँगला' में
'हजार बिछोर धोरे आमी पोथ हेयंटी तै छी, प्रथवीर पोथे . . . '
किसी बादल ने चेहरा ढाँप रक्खा है
नज़र आती हैं लेकिन दो सिया आँखें
'मोने पोड़े नाटोरे बनलता सेन !'

Someone is between the rails, approaching,
Reading a *nazm* in Bangla
'*hazar bachur dhore, ami poth payanti te chi, prithvir pothe*'
For a thousand years I have walked the paths of this earth.

A cloud has obscured his face
But two shining dark eyes can be clearly seen
'*Moun pode natore Banalata sen*'
Reminds one of Banalata Sen of Natur.

पाब्लो नेरूदा

ज़र्रा ज़र्रा से लम्हे कमाल पकड़ते हैं।
नज़्म का पहला हिस्सा उनका है। दूसरा मेरा।

पाब्लो नेरूदा

कभी कभी पाब्लो की बात सही लगती हैं
'नज़्में बाऊँस्ड चेक होती हैं!'
जिसके लिये लिखी थी उसने . . .
पढ़ के गर्दन को हल्का सा ख़म देकर,
इतना ही कहा था
'अच्छी है!' और लौटा दी थी!

कभी कभी लिक्खा होता है
चेक दोबारा पेश करो!
मजमूये में आई तो, दोबारा उसको पेश किया
अब की बार ज़रा सा होंट दबा कर वो मुस्काई, लेकिन . . .
हम दोनों तब उम्र के दूसरे हिस्से में थे!

Pablo Neruda

He could catch the slightest nuances of a moment, so wonderfully.
The first quotes of the poem are his. The second part, mine.

Pablo . . .!

Often I feel there is truth in what Pablo says,
'A poem is a bounced cheque.'
The one I wrote it for
Read it, inclined her head slightly and said,
'It's good,' and returned it.

Sometimes, it's written,
'Present the cheque again!'
When published in my book, I presented it again.
This time, slightly biting her lip, she smiled, but . . .
By then, we were both in the second half of our lives.

फ़ैज़ अहमद फ़ैज़

ज़िंदन नामा

चाँद लाहौर की गलियों से गुज़र के इक शब
जेल की ऊँची फ़सीलें जढ़ के
यूँ 'कमान्डो' की तरह कूद गया था 'सेल' में
कोई आहट न हुई
पेहरेदारों को पता ही न चला।

'फ़ैज़' से मिलने गया था, ये सुना है
'फ़ैज़' से कहने, कोई नज़्म कहो
वक़्त की नब्ज़ रुकी है
कुछ कहो
वक़्त की नब्ज़ चले!

Faiz Ahmad Faiz

Zindan Nama

Traversing the lanes of Lahore one night,
Scaling the high reaches of the jail's wall, the moon
Jumped with such commando-like stealth into the cell
That there was no sound.
The guards remained unaware.

It's said that it went to meet Faiz,
To tell him, 'Write a poem,
Time's pulse has stopped beating,
Recite something
That Time's pulse may throb again.'

नाज़िम हिकमत

नाज़िम ने कहा था !

नाज़िम ने कहा था . . . नाज़िम हिकमत ने
'मुझको जला के, राख मेरी, इक मर्तबान में
आतिशदान पे रख देना . . .'
ये सोच के शायद
आतिशदान में आग रहे
तुम ऊन के मोज़े बुन्ती रहो
चुपचाप मैं सामने सोया रहूँ !

अब सोचता हूँ, मैं तुम से कहूँ
गमले में अगर रख दोगी मुझे . . .
इक फूल पकड़ के बैठा रहूँगा,
जब भी वहाँ से गुज़रोगी !

Nazim Hikmet

SO SAID NAZIM

Nazim had said . . . Nazim Hikmet
'When I die, burn my body
And place my ashes in a jar
And put me on the mantlepiece in your room.'
Perhaps thinking that
The fireplace will be alight
And sitting beside it, you will be knitting socks
While I sit quietly opposite you.

Now I think I should tell you,
If you place me in a flowerpot
I will sit holding out a flower,
Each time you pass by.

सुखबीर

पँजाबी के बड़े शायर थे।

शायरी के इलावा कहानियाँ और नोवेल भी लिखे। हमारी मुलाक़ात 50 के दौर में हुई थी। पँजाबी साहित्य सभा में। और फिर PWA में। ख़ासा जुनून हम दोनों का शायरी में ही था। 2012 में उनका इंतेक़ाल हुआ। आख़िर आख़िर तक हम एक दूसरे के राब्ते (contact) में रहे। साठ साल की तवील दोस्ती, एक लँबा सफ़र था . . . मुझसे बड़ा था। तो क्या? पहले जाने की क्या जल्दी थी।

सुखबीर

छड़ी थी शायरी की हाथ में
चलता था जब, आवाज़ होती थी
गुरू था, शख़्सियत में माहिरे-फ़न गूँजता था
सिखाता था . . .
न समझो गर तो चुप रह कर ज़रा सा मुस्कुराता था
छड़ी आवाज़ करती थी
सियाही की महक थी उसके बोलों में
क़लम की टहनी से वो आसमाँ को 'पेंट' करता था

Sukhbir

He was a renowned poet of Punjab. Authored stories and novels too, besides writing poetry. We met sometime in the 1950s; at the Punjabi Sahitya Sabha, and then at the PWA. Our poems reflected our special passions. He passed away in 2012. We remained in contact till the very end. A friendship spanning sixty years, it was a long journey indeed. He was older than me . . . but so what? Where was the hurry to be the first to go?

Sukhbir

He held the staff of poetry in his hand
It resounded whenever he walked about
His personality sparkled with his masterful art
He was a teacher—

If you did not understand him, he would softly smile
But his staff would resound.
His words were scented with the fragrance of ink
He would paint the sky with the stem of his pen.

क़दम रखता था जब तो उसके पैरों की धमक से
किताबें खुलने लगती थीं
न जाने किस तरफ़ निकला है वो अपनी क़लम लेकर
किताबें फड़फड़ाती हैं
छड़ी के बजने की आवाज़ आती है !

Whenever he walked, then,

The sound of his feet would make books fly open,

Don't know in which direction he is headed, pen in hand

The books are all a-flutter

The sound of his staff can be heard.

ग्रेस

मराठी ज़बान के बड़े ख़ुद्दार, मोडर्न शायर थे। हम एक दूसरे की शायरी का बहुत एहतराम करते थे। ग़ायबाना तारुफ़ काफ़ी लँबा था लेकिन आख़िर आख़िर में हम बहुत क़रीब आ गये। वो कैंसर की आख़री स्टेज से गुज़र रहे थे, जब मुलाक़ातें कुछ बढ़ गयीं। और वो आख़री मुलाक़ात हमेशा याद रहेगी।

'मेरे कह देने से रुक जाओगे, ऐसा तो नहीं है!'

ग्रेस

मेरे कह देने से रुक जाओगे, ऐसा तो नहीं है!

अपना सामाने सफ़र बाँध रहे हो,
जो तुम्हें छोड़ के जाना है यहीं!
शीशियाँ बँद हुई नज़्मों की और कॉर्क (cork) लगा कर . . .
'ख़त्म शुद' मोहर लगा दी तुमने
जो तुम्हें कहना था वो कह भी चुके
और कोई अर्ज़ नहीं, मोज़र्त कोई नहीं
'नंगी तलवारें मुझे पीठ में चुभने लगी हैं' ये कहा था
नंगी तलवारों पे ये किसने लिटाया है तुम्हें?

Grace

He was a very independent-minded, modern Marathi poet. We had deep respect for each other's poetry. Our relationship was a long-distance one for a long time, but towards the end we got very close to each other. Our meetings grew more frequent when he was going through the last stages of cancer. And I will forever remember that last meeting:

'I ask you to stay, and you stay . . . that cannot be!'

Grace

I ask you to stay and you stay . . . that cannot be!
You are packing for a journey,
Things you have to leave behind.
The vials that hold poems are sealed . . .
You corked them all
And stamped 'the end' on them.
You have said what you had to say
No plea or excuse now remains
'Naked swords are pushi g their points into my back'
You said,
'Who laid you down on a bed of swords?'

'पकड़े जाते हैं फ़रिश्तों के लिखे पर नाहक़
आदमी कोई हमारा दमे तहरीर भी था?' (ग़ालिब)

'Pakde jaate hain fariston ke likhe par nahak
Admi koi hamara dame tehrir bhi tha?'
'We are punished for reports of the angels
Was there any human being to vouch for us?'

ग्रेस

हम दोनों ही इस बात से आगा थे ग्रेस
तुम उसी रात चले जाओगे, या . . . कल शायद!
चौबदार, मौत का साया, बहुत पास कहीं, टहल रहा था!

तुम भी कुछ शेर सुनाते रहे और मैं भी . . .
दोनों इस बात से डरते थे कि ख़ामोश हुए तो,
अलविदा कहना पड़े ना
और वो आख़िरी होगा!

क्या कहूँगा जब उठूँ . . . हाथ छुड़ा कर?
क्या कहोगे भला तुम, चलते हुए?
हाथ पकड़े हुए कुछ माज़ी की सीढ़ियाँ चढ़ कर
कुछ गुज़रता मुलाक़ातों पे फिस्ले और उठे
तुमने जब अपनी तरह कह ही दिया:
'अब के आओ तो नई नज़्म भी लेकर आना!'

नज़्म लाया हूँ 'ग्रेस' . . . सुनोगे?

Grace

Both of us could foretell for sure, Grace,
You would leave that same night, or tomorrow, perhaps
Holding his mace, the shadow of death
Was hovering somewhere close!

You kept reciting poems, I too,
Both afraid of the fact that falling silent
Would mean saying goodbye
The last one.

What will I say when I rise . . . releasing your hand
What would you say, as you leave?

Hand in hand we had climbed some memory's steps
Slipping and steadying on some meetings past
When in your fashion you finally said,
'When next you come, bring along a new poem.'

I have brought a poem, Grace. Will you listen?

नामदेव ढसाल

मैंने किसी शायर के जनाज़े पर इतनी भीड़ अवाम की नहीं देखी। कभी नहीं! नामदेव की शायरी में जो शिद्दत थी, वो उसकी चिता की आग भी राख न कर सकी। वो अवाम का शायर था। और दलित तहरीक का अल्मबर्दार। अल्मबर्दार कहते हैं flag holder को! नामदेव से जब भी मुलाकात हुई हमेशा लिट्रेचर की, और दूसरे शायरों, या अदीबों की। बहुत कम हुआ कि हमने अपनी नज़्में कभी एक दूसरे को सुनायी हों।

कोई रोज़ का मिलना नहीं था। लेकिन नामदेव जब गये, एक बड़ी ख़ला का एहसास हुआ।

नामदेव ढसाल

कुछ घूम कर आना पड़ा था, इस लिये—
उम्र लग गयी
हालाँकि, मेरे घर से भी शमशान बहुत दूर नहीं था!

काला सफ़ेद, लँबी चौड़ी इक बिसात थी
फ़ीले थे, हाथी, घोड़े, और कुछ हुक्मरान थे
और उनके आगे पीछे कुछ पियादे मेरी तरह
पहला क़दम उठाया तो . . . चिरा हुआ था मैं!

Namdeo Dhasal

I have not seen such a crowd of people at any other poet's funeral. Never ever! Even the flames from his pyre could not reduce the intensity of his poetry to ashes. He was the people's poet. A flag holder for the Dalit cause. Whenever we would meet we would discuss literature or other poets. It was rarely that we recited our poems to each other. It was not as if we met every day. Yet, when he went, I felt a great vacuum.

Namdeo Dhasal

The path was circuitous, that is why
It took me an age to arrive
Though, in fact, even from my house
The cremation ground was not quite so far.

Black and white, long and wide
A chessboard;
Spread on it, bishops, elephants, horses, some rulers
And ahead of them, and behind, some footmen
Like me . . .
I had just taken my first step, but was surrounded.

जिसने खड़ा किया था मुझको इस बिसात पर
कुछ गैंडे से कलाईयों में बाँध दिये थे
पहले से कुछ अक़ीदों की हथकड़ियाँ डाल दीं
पाबंदियाँ बता दीं मुझको, मेरी चाल की !

इतने ज़यादा पैरों के निशान थे बिसात पर
मेरे लिये तो, पाँव रखने की जगह न थी
चलता किधर ? . . . जाता कहाँ ?

धमकियाँ धकेलती रहीं कहीं
कहीं पे ख़ौफ़ ने भगा लिया
ख़ुदा मिले कई, कई जगह,
कँधे पे हाथ रखके जब दबाते थे
तो हड्डी दर्द करने लगती थी
जीने से ज़्यादा सब ख़ुदाओं को
आक़िबत की फ़िक्र रहती थी !
ज़िंदगी में—
ज़िन्दा रहने की कोई भी चाल नहीं थी !

शायद मैं ग़लत राह पर निकल गया
वरना तो, घर से ये शमशान बहुत दूर नहीं था !

They, who had placed me on this chessboard
Had tied charms on to my wrists
Already they had handcuffed me in doctrines,
Told me of restrictions to my movements.

So many footprints on the chessboard
There was no space for me to place my foot
Where would I walk? Where would I go?

Threats pushed me here and there
At times fear took me on a run
Many Gods I met, in many places
When they'd place their hands on my shoulders
And press down, my very bones would hurt
Every God more worried about hell and heaven
Than life itself.
In life . . .
There was no way to stay alive.

Maybe I started out on the wrong path
Otherwise, the cremation ground was not too far from my house.

सत्यपाल आनंद

हिंदूस्तान और पाकिस्तान के तक़रीबन हर अहम उर्दू रिसालों में अब तक मुतवातिर शाय होते रहते हैं। कई रिसालों में पास पास नज़्में छपीं। ख़ूसूसन 'फ़नून' में, और पास पास छपते छपते एक दिन आमने सामने आ गये . . . अमरीका में! तब से मुसलसल राबता रहता है! राबता मतलब contact!

उर्दू की शायरी में space और सितारों की बातें सिर्फ़ उन्हीं के साथ होती हैं। उनकी पैदाइश भी पाकिस्तान की है।

सत्यपाल आनंद

छुट्टी के दिन . . .
सत्यपाल आनंद और मैं
'कोसमोस' जेबों में भर कर
अक्सर चाँद के पीछे वाले आसमान में जाकर खेला करते हैं

सात सितारे ऊपर के,
दो नीचे रखके,
नौ पत्थर का पिट्ठू खेलना
'क्रिमिच' वाली चाँद की गेंद को उतार के ले जाया करते हैं

Satyapal Anand

He is regularly published in almost every Urdu magazine in India and Pakistan. In many magazines, our poems were published next to each other. Especially, in *Fanoon* this happened quite frequently. And with our poems being thus published in proximity, one day, we came face to face . . . in America. After that, we continue to remain in constant contact.

He alone, among all Urdu poets, talks with me on space and stars. He was born in Pakistan.

Satyapal Anand

On holidays, Satyapal Anand and I
Fill our pockets with 'Cosmos'
And, in the sky behind the moon,
We go to play.

Seven stars plucked from above
Two placed below them . . .
To break open the pack of nine stones
We would take down the moon
And use as the ball.

कभी कभी अंटी होती है
ये वीनस का कँचा है,
और वो जुपिटर का बँटा!

गिल्ली डँडा भी जमता है
चल कोमेट का डँडा लेकर
'शू मेकर' की गिल्ली से
गिल्ली डँडा खेलेंगे!

इतनी ज़ोर न मारियो गिल्ली
काँच ज़मीं का टूट गया तो
फ़िश टेंक की सारी मच्छियाँ स्पेस में गिर के मर जायेंगी!
और बड़े मियाँ से डाँट पड़ेगी!

Sometimes it would be marbles,
This is Venus as the shooter
And that, the 'duck', is Jupiter.

Gilli-danda is also possible
With Hailey Comet's tail as *'danda'*
And 'Shoemaker' as the *'gilli'*
Let us play the game.

Do not hit the 'gilli' so hard
If Earth's glassy surface breaks, then
All the fish in the fish tank, will fall into space
And die.
And the 'Old Man' will give us a scolding.

कुसुमाग्रज

पूरे नाम से दुनिया वाक़िफ़ है। वि.वि.शिरवाडकर (V.V. Shirwadkar)। ज़्यादा काम तो 'नसर' में किया—फ़िक्शन में। 'नाटया सम्राट' उनका ड्रामा। हिंदुस्तान की तक़रीबन हर ज़बान में उसका ज़िक्र मौजूद है। लेकिन वो जो ज़िंदगी के छोटे छोटे लम्हों पर नज़्में कहीं, उनका सफ़र बहुत लँबा है। आज़ादी की तहरीक से जुड़े रहे। आज़ादी के बाद भी।

जब भी मिला उन्हें . . . एक नया उत्साह लेकर लौटा। एक नयी Inspiration!

कुसुमाग्रज

कल रात जो पुल के ऊपर से देखा तो, नीचे
जाती हुई कारों की लाल दहक्ती बत्तियाँ दूर तलक
सुर्ख़ दहक्ते कोयेलों जैसी लगती थीं
हर साल मोहर्रम में जिन पर
मैं नंगे पाँव चलता हूँ!

'कुसुमाग्रज' के पाँव में छाले पड़ जाते थे
लाल गुलाब की पत्तियों पर जब चलता था
आज़ादी की तहरीक के शोले याद आते थे!

Kusumagraj

The world knows him by his full name, V.V. Shirwadkar. Mostly he wrote in prose; wrote fiction. His play 'Nat-Samrat' has been referred to in writings in every Indian language. But the poems he wrote about the infinitesimal moments of life will continue to resonate for long. He was involved in the freedom struggle. Even after Independence.

Whenever I would meet him, I would return with a new excitement . . . a new inspiration!

Kusumagraj

Last night as I looked down from the bridge,
The tail lights of the cars as they drove away
Smouldered like the burning embers of coal
On which I walk with bare feet
Every year, on Muharram.

Kusumagraj's feet would sprout blisters
When he would walk on the petals of red roses
The burning flames of Independence would come to mind.

केदारनाथ सिंह

हिंदी के बड़े कवि। बड़े शायर। हँसमुख इंसान। कश्मीरियों की सी चेहरे की रँगत हमेशा सुर्ख़ रहती थी। लगता था कोई गुदगुदी दबाये हुए हैं। छेड़ दिया तो हँसी फूट पड़ेगी।

मेरा एक गीत 'हमको मन की शक्ती देना, मन विजय करें' छपा देख कर बोले, 'ये भी तुम्हारा लिखा है? ये तो स्कूलों में गाया जाता है!' मैंने सर झुकाके स्वीकार किया तो कहा 'बड़े ख़ुश क़िस्मत हो। तुम्हारा काम, तुम्हारे नाम से आगे निकल गया!'

केदारनाथ सिंह

तुम्हारे बाद एक दिन—
तुम्हारे नाम की एक चिट्ठी आई है
कहीं पे तुम किसी के वास्ते
अभी भी ज़िंदा हो!

तुम्हारे नाम से उसे जवाब दे दिया
कहीं भी हो—कहीं पे तो
ज़िंदा हो अभी तलक—

Kedarnath Singh

A big name in Hindi poetry. A renowned poet. A cheerful person. His face always had a healthy freshness like the faces of Kashmiri people. It seemed as if something was secretly tickling him. And the slightest provocation could cause the laughter to burst forth.

Seeing a song of mine, '*Hum ko man ki shanti dena, man vijay karen*', in print, he said, 'Is this also written by you? This is sung in schools.' I bowed my head in acceptance. Then, he said, 'What a lucky man you are! Your work has outstripped your name.'

Kedarnath Singh

After you had gone, one day
A letter has come in your name
Somewhere, for someone
You are even now alive.

I replied to it, in your name
Wherever you are—somewhere
You are alive still.

कुछ और दिन इसी मुबालग़े में जी लूँ मैं
कि तुम अभी गये नहीं
यहीं कहीं पे हो !

Some more days let me live
In the exaggerated belief
That you have not gone
But are here, somewhere.

अंजल

गीतांजली नाम था उस लड़की का। उस एक फ़ोन के इलावा मेरी कोई वाक़्फ़ियत न थी उस लड़की से। उस फ़ोन के डेढ़ दो साल बाद उनकी अम्मी से तारुफ़ हुआ तो पता चला कि वाक़्यी वो उसकी आख़िरी दो तीन रातों में से एक थी। वो कैंसर की लास्ट स्टेज पर थी। और उम्र कुल चौधा बरस की थी।

एक माँगे हुए वादे की तरह, वो रात अब भी कभी कभी याद आ जाती है।

अंजल

नींद की चादर चीर के बाहर निकला था मैं
आधी रात इक फ़ोन बजा था . . .

दूर किसी सिरे से
इक अनजान आवाज़ ने छू कर पूछा था:
'आप ही वो शायर हैं जिसने
अपनी कुछ नज़्में "सोना" के नाम लिखी हैं?
मेरा नाम भी "सोना" हो तो?'

इक पतली सी झिल्ली जैसी ख़ामोशी का लँबा वक़्फ़ा।
'मेरे नाम इक नज़्म लिखो नां!
मुझको अपने इक छोटे से शेर में सी दो,
"अंजल" लिखना . . .
शायद मेरी आख़री शब है

Anjal

The girl's name was Geetanjali. I had no acquaintance with her, beyond a phone call. When about a year-and-a-half or two years after that call, I was introduced to her mother, I learnt that indeed, that night had been among the last few of her life. She had been in the last stages of cancer. And had been about fourteen years old.

Like a promise made under pressure, that night still sometimes haunts my memory.

Anjal

Tearing apart the sheets of sleep, I had emerged
The phone had rung in the middle of the night;
From far away, an unknown voice touched me and asked,
'Are you the poet who has written a few poems
dedicating them to Sona?
What if my name is Sona too?'

A long silence stretching like a thin membrane . . .
'Write a poem in my name, *na*,
Sew me into one of your short couplets
Write, "Anjal"
Perhaps it's my last night

आख़री ख़्वाहिश है, मैं आपको सौंप के जाऊँ?'
फोन बुझाकर . . .
धज्जी धज्जी नींद में फिर जा लेटा था मैं!

अंजल!
इसके बहुत दिनों के बाद मुझे मालूम हुआ था
दर्द से दर्द बुझाने की इक कोशिश में तुम,
कैंसर की उस आग में मेरी नज़्में छिड़का करती थीं . . .

नींद भरी रात कभी याद आये तो,
अब भी ऐसा होता है
एक धुआँ सा आँखों में भर जाता है!

My last desire. Can I bequeath it to you and go?'
I had snuffed the phone
And returned to bed.

Anjal!
Months after this I came to know,
Trying to quell pain with pain, you
Would sprinkle my poems on cancer's raging fire.

Whenever that sleep-drenched night comes to mind
I feel even now
Something like smoke filling my eyes.

सुक्रीता

अँग्रेज़ी की बेशुमार किताबों की मुसन्निफ़ हैं। बहुत पढ़ती हैं और पढ़ाती हैं। किसी रिसर्च के काम में मसरूफ़ रहती हैं . . . उसके बावजूद शायरी भी करती हैं। पेन्टिंग भी! सिर्फ़ अपने वालिद की तरह कहानियाँ नहीं लिखतीं। उर्दू के बहुत मशहूर अफ़साना निगार 'जोगिंदर पाल' की बेटी हैं!

दिल्ली में मेरी शाम की ड्रिंक्स और डिनर हमेशा उन्हीं के साथ होता है। जहाँ जाना हो, वही ड्राईव करती हैं, इसलिये, ये नज़्म हुई जो आप पढ़ रहे हैं!

'मुझे मालूम है तुम रास्ते क्यों भूल जाती हो!'

सुक्रीता

मुझे मालूम है तुम रास्ते क्यों भूल जाती हो!

तुम्हें हर रास्ते के अंत से डर लगने लगता है
कोई भी रास्ते जो देर तक सीधा चला जाये
तुम्हें लगता है ये भी . . .
न पहुँचेगा कहीं,
या बंद हो जायेगा आख़िर में
यही अच्छा है कोई मोड़ मुड़ जाओ!

तुम्हें कुछ रास्ते दोहराने से भी ख़ौफ़ आता है
कि तुम हर जाने पहचाने हुए रस्ते से डरती हो

Sukrita

The author of many a book in English. Reads a lot and is a professor too. Is always immersed in some research or the other . . . despite which she writes poetry. Paints too. Only, unlike her father, she does not write stories. She is the daughter of the renowned Urdu fiction writer, Joginder Pal.

While in Delhi, my drinks and dinner are with them. If we have to go somewhere, she drives. Hence the poem that you will read below.

'I know why you forget your way on the roads.'

Sukrita

I know why you forget your way on the roads

You have started being afraid of the roads' ending
Any road that stretches straight for long
You feel this too
Will not reach anywhere
Or reach a dead end somewhere;
Better then, that I take a turn somewhere.

You dread too, to repeat the roads once taken
In fact you fear every road that you are familiar with.

कई बार हो चुका है बेध्यानी में
उसी दरवाज़े पर आकर रुकी हो, और
दस्तक देते देते बच गये हो
कि जो अंधी गली का आख़री घर था!
मुझे मालूम है तुम रास्ते क्यों भूल जाती हो!

Often times it has been that unmindfully
You have come to stop at the same door
The last house at the end of the dead end lane
And saved yourself from knocking in the nick of time.

I know why you forget your way on the roads.

अरुण शेवटे

मराठी के ऊँचे दरजे के शायर और सहाफ़ी हैं। सहाफ़ी यानी जर्नलिस्ट। मेरा मराठी ज़बान के लेखन से जितना भी रिश्ता है वो इन्हीं की बदौलत है। नम्रता से भरपूर और निहायत बेग़रज़ इंसान हैं . . . वो एक ही शख़्स हैं, जिन्हें मैंने ज़िंदगी भर के लिये सुबह आठ बजे का वक़्त दे रखा है। जब चाहें चले आयें। रात को आठ बजे मिलें तो cheers के लिये मिलते हैं!

अरुण शेवटे

तुम्हारे साथ अरुण, अक्सर मैं भटका हूँ
घने शहरों में जाकर
ज़िंदगी की पत्ता पत्ता बूटा देखा है
जड़ें ढूँढीं हैं लोगों में
सभी के दर्द दरज करते रहे हैं
मगर देखा . . .
दवा भी थे वही, जो दर्द थे इस ज़िंदगी के!

Arun Shevate

A very highly regarded Marathi poet and journalist. Whatever relationship I have with Marathi is thanks to him. Full of gentleness and an extremely unbiased soul . . . he is the only person to whom I have given the time of eight o' clock in the morning, for the rest of my life, as a time to meet. He can come whenever he feels like it. And if he should walk in at eight at night, then we meet to say 'cheers'.

Arun Shevate

Oft have I wandered with you, Arun,
In thronging cities,
Seen the minute intricacies of life,
Searched in people, plumbing for their roots,
Recorded every single hurt and woe
Then realized that,
In the agonies of life itself, lay their healing remedies.

जावेद अख़तर

एक लड़की को देखा तो ऐसा लगा!

बड़ा अच्छा लगा मिल कर
मेरी मदाह थी, इक फ़ेन थी मेरी
वो मेरी शायरी की ख़ूबियाँ पहचानती थी
मेरे मिसरे, मेरी तश्बीहें, उसके दिल को छूती थीं
मुझे मिल कर अचानक बौखलाने लग गयी थी
बड़ी नर्वस हँसी हँस कर कहा:
'मुझे डर है मैं अपना नाम ही नां भूल जाऊँ!'
बग़लगीर हो के मोबाईल पे इक तस्वीर भी ली
गयी तो नाम लेकर 'शुक्रीया' कह कर गयी वो . . .
वो मेरा नाम न था!

हमेशा से यही डर था . . .
कि वो कमबख़्त मुझ से अच्छा लिखता है!

Javed Akhtar

EK LADKI KO DEKHA TOH AISA LAGA . . .

It felt so good meeting her
Singing my praises, she was my fan
She understood the merits of my poetry
My imagery, my similes, touched her heart.
On meeting me, she was suddenly flustered
Laughing nervously she said,
'I just . . . might forget . . . my own name.'
She took a selfie as she embraced me
And left after thanking me, taking my name . . .
That was not my name!

This has always been my fear
That rascal writes better than me.

जयन्त महापात्रा

मैंने शायर की मौत का तसव्वुर करते हुए एक नज़्म लिखी थी। ये एक अन्थालोजी में भी शाये हुआ था। लेकिन जब मैंने जयन्त महापात्र की मौत की ख़बर सुनी तो नज़्म को अपना घर मिल गया!

जयन्त महापात्रा

वो जो शायर था, चुप सा रहता था
बहकी बहकी सी बातें करता था
आँखें कानों पे रखके सुनता था
गूँगी ख़ामोशियों की आवाज़ें!
जमा करता था चाँद के साये
गीली गीली सी नूर की बूँदें
ओक में भर के खड़खड़ाता था
रूखे रूखे से रात के पत्ते
वक़्त के इस घनेरे जंगल में
कच्चे पक्के से लम्हे चुन्ता था!

Jayanta Mahapatra

I had written a poem imagining the death of a poet. It was published in an anthology. But when I heard of Jayanta Mahapatra's death, the poem found its home.

Jayanta Mahapatra

He who was a poet, often held his silence
Often spoke his wandering thoughts

He would listen with his eyes intently
As his ears caught the sounds of mute voices

He would collect the shadows of the moon
And droplets of light, somewhat damp

Holding in his palm, he would rattle
The leaves of the night

Pick from the dense forest of time
Moments that were raw, moments that were ripe

हाँ, वही, वो अजीब सा शायर
रात को उठके कोहनियों के बल
चाँद की ठोड़ी चूमा करता था!

कल सुना है ज़मीं से उठ गया है वो!

Yes, he, that strange poet
Who, waking at night, would raise himself on his elbows
To kiss the moon's chin

He has abandoned the earth
I heard, yesterday.

II

बिमलदा

बिमलदा मेरे गुरू थे। फ़िल्म के अदब उन्हीं से सीखा। वो अगर हाथ पकड़ के उठा न लेते, तो पता नहीं और कितने साल उसी मोटर गैरिज में काम करता।

नि‍हायत संजीदा इंसान! सारी फ़िक्र एक चुप में छुपाये रखते थे। बहुत कम बोलते थे। लबों पर सिर्फ़ एक 'हूं' और एक जलता हुआ सिग्रेट!

बिमलदा: पोट्रेट

शाम के कोहरे में बहता हुआ ख़ामोश नदी का चेहरा
गंदुमी कोहरे में जलते हुए आँखों के चिराग़
इक लगातार सुलगता हुआ सिग्रेट का धुआँ
नींद में डूबी हुई दूर की मध्दम आवाज़

अजनबी ख्वाबों के उड़ते हुए सायों के तले
मोम की तरह पिघलते हुए चेहरे के नक़ूश
हर नये ख्वाब की धुन सुनके बदल जाते हैं
ऐसा लगता है न सोयेगा, न जागेगा, न बोलेगा कभी
शाम के कोहरे में बहता हुआ ख़ामोश नदी का चेहरा!

Bimal Da

Bimal Da was my guru. I learnt all the discipline of film-making from him. If he had not taken me by the hand, who knows how many years more I would have continued to work in the same motor garage.

A very contained personality. Would hide all his worries in a wrapped silence. He spoke sparsely. Only a 'hun' and a burning cigarette on his lips.

Bimal Roy: A Portrait

The softly flowing river face shrouded in the evening mists
Eyes burning in the mistiness of a tawny visage
The spiral of smoke from the endlessly burning cigarette
The faraway voice heavy with sleep.

Shadowed below unknown thoughts that flew above
A face that seemed etched out of molten wax
The sound of every new dream transforms him
Making it seem he would neither sleep, nor wake, nor speak
A silent flowing river shrouded in evening mists.

नसीरुद्दीन शाह

ऐक्ट्रस को मौज़ू और कहानी के मुताबिक़, 'गेटअप' और पोशाकें बदलते हमेशा देखा है मैंने। लेकिन जिस्म का पूरा ढाँचा बदलते हुए मैंने सिर्फ़ इसी एक्टर को देखा है। मसलन 'पीस्टनजी', 'स्पर्श' और ग़ालिब में तीन एक्टर नज़र आते हैं। एक नसीर नज़र नहीं आते। ऐक्टिंग को शौक़ और प्रोफ़ेशन के इलावा एक आर्ट और स्किल समझ कर, उसका मुताला करना इसी शख़्स में देखा है। शौक़ इतना कि वो अब तक सीख रहा है और सीखने को तैयार है।

मेरी ज़िंदगी का बहतरीन काम, 'ग़ालिब' उन्हीं की बदोलत मुमकिन हो सका।

नसीरुद्दीन शाह

इक अदाकार हूँ मैं!
मैं अदाकार हूँ नां
जीनी पड़ती है कई ज़िंदगियाँ एक हयाती में मुझे!

मेरा किर्दार बदल जाता है, हर रोज़ ही सेट पर
मेरे हालात बदल जाते हैं
मेरा चेहरा भी बदल जाता है, अफ़साना-व-मँज़र के मुताबिक़
मेरी आदत बदल जाती है
और फिर दाग़ नहीं छूटते पहनी हुई पोशाकों के

Naseeruddin Shah

I have seen actors change their get-up and costumes as the milieu and storyline dictates. But I have seen only one actor who changes the entire demeanour of his bearing and his body language each time. For example, we see three distinctly different people in Pestonji, Sparsh and Ghalib, rather than one Naseer. I have realized that for him acting goes beyond being a profession or a passion; it is an art that has to be interpreted with skill. And such is his passion that he is still learning it, with a keen willingness to continue learning.

I owe it to him that Ghalib, the best work of my life, is considered the finest of my creations.

Naseeruddin Shah

A performer am I
Yet not just an actor
But one who must live
Many lifetimes in one life.

My persona changes, each day on the set
My circumstances change.
My looks change too, to match story and spectacle,
My habits I change, and then,
I cannot rid myself of the stains my garbs leave on my skin.

ख़स्ता किर्दारों का कुछ चुरा सा रह जाता है तह में
कोई नोकीला सा किर्दार गुज़रता है रगों से तो ख़राशों
के निशाँ देर तलक रहते हैं दिल पर
ज़िंदगी से ये उठाये हुए किर्दार ख़्याली भी नहीं हैं कि उतर
जायें वो पँखे की हवा से

सियाही रह जाती है सीने में, अदीबों के लिखे जुमलों की
सेमी पर्दें पे लिखी
साँस लेती हुई तहरीर नज़र आता है

मैं अदाकार हूँ लेकिन
सिर्फ़ अदाकार नहीं
वक़्त की तस्वीर भी हूँ!

The remnants of fragile characters linger in my depths
Sharp-edged characters flow through my veins
To leave wounds that scar my heart for days on end.
Carved out of real life these characters that I play,
Cannot, as imaginary ones would, be blown away
With a turning of the fan.

The ink pools in my heart; I am the breathing image
Who on the unbleached screen can be seen
Living out the lines written by creative minds.

A performer am I
But not just an actor
I am also a mirror of Time.

बासू . . . बासू भट्टाचार्य

हम दोनों गुरू भाई थे। फ़िल्म आर्ट दोनों ने बिमलदा से सीखा था। बहुत बातूनी था। पेट भर के बोलता था। उसकी बात कभी ख़त्म ही नहीं होती थी। यही हाल था उसकी नज़्मों का भी . . . बात से बात निकलती ही चली जाती थी। पर बड़ा मज़ा आता था उसकी बातों का। एक ज़रा सा दर्द हुआ पेट में और उठा के हस्ताल ले गये उसे।

डाक्टरों ने पेट ही ख़ाली कर दिया उसका। चुप करा दिया ! बहुत अज़ीज़ एक दोस्त चला गया।

बासू

हस्पताल ले गये थे उसको हम
दर्द होता था उसे
पेट में . . . कभी कभी
दर्द होता था तो नाग की तरह वो अपना
सारा जिस्म पेट में लपेट लेता था
साँस फूल जाती थी
ख़ून का दबाओ तेज़ रहता था

Basu . . . Basu Bhattacharya

We were both students of the same guru, *guru-bhais*. Both of us learnt the art of film-making from Bimal Da. He was a chatterbox. With a stomachful of talk. His talking would never end. It was the same with his poems too. One thing would lead to another and it would just keep going on. But it was great fun to listen to him talking.

A mild stomachache, and we took him to the hospital. The doctors emptied his stomach completely. Silenced him. I lost a dear friend.

Basu

We had taken him to the hospital
A stomachache would assail him
At times.
When the pain would strike, like a serpent
He would wrap himself around his stomach
His breath would accelerate
And the blood thunder in his veins.

हस्पताल में
डॉक्टरों ने 'ऐप्रन' पहन के
और पेट खोल के,
साफ़ कर के सारे ज़ख़्म, और दर्द को
जड़ों से काट के
फिर से 'पैक' कर दिया
जिस्म का वो ख़ौल ला के हस्पताल से
चिता पे रखके, आग में जला दिया!

The hospital doctors donning their aprons
Opened his stomach
Cleaned out the debris, and cutting the roots of his pain
'Packed' him up again.

Bringing the shell of that body from the hospital
We placed it on the pyre
And burnt it.

जगजीत सिंह

मशहूर गायक—ग़ज़ल का मिज़ाज उनमें इस तरह भरा हुआ था जैसे हिरन की नाभी में कस्थूरी!
मैं अक्सर उन्हें 'ग़ज़लजीत सिंह' भी कह लिया करता था। ख़ुश दिल, ख़ुश मिज़ाज इंसान। मेरा
पड़ोसी भी और मेरी शामों का हिस्सेदार भी . . . बहुत रसीला आदमी था। छोटा मुझसे। लाईन
तोड़ के जल्दी निकल गया।

शाम से आँख में नमी सी है
आज फिर आपकी कमी सी है

जगजीत सिंह

एक बोछार था वो—
एक बोछार था वो शख़्स, बिना बरसे किसी अबर की
सहमी सी नमी से जो भिगो देता था—
एक बोछार था वो, जो कभी धूप की अफ़शाँ भर के
दूर तक, सुनते हुए चेहरों पे छिड़क देता था
नीम तारीक़ से हाल में आँखें चमक उठती थीं

Jagjit Singh

A renowned singer. The spirit of the ghazal had settled in him like musk in the depths of a deer. I would often allude to him as Ghazaljit Singh. A happy-go-lucky man with a sunny temperament. My neighbour, whom I often shared my evenings with. A man with a lust for life. He was younger than me. But broke the queue and left early.

A wetness resides in the eyes since evening
Something like your absence is felt again today

Jagjit Singh

Like a cool spray he was,
That without raining like a cloud
Carried a hidden moisture
To envelop you in its mist.

He was just a fresh spray,
Which sometimes gathering flecks of sunlight
Would sprinkle it on listeners' faces all around
Lighting up their eyes in the dusky twilight.

सर हिलाता था कभी झूम के टहनी की तरह,
लगता था झोंका हवा का था कोई छेड़ गया है
गुनगुनाता था तो खुलते हुए बादल की तरह
मुस्कुराहट में कई तरबों की झनकार छुपी थी
गली क़ासिम से चली एक ग़ज़ल की झनकार था वो
एक आवाज़ की बोछार था वो!

Often he would shake his head, a branch
Teased by a breath of passing breeze
Like the spreading cloud, his humming rose
His smiles echoed with the sound of strings
A ghazal trailing down Gali Quasim was he
A spray of melody he was . . .

जगजीत सिंह: मर्सिया नोहा

जाने कैसी सर्दी आके बैठ गयी थी
जम गयी थी उसके सीने में
ग़ज़ल की काँगड़ी जला के पहन लेता था

बेटे को जला के लौटा तो . . .
झील किनारे बैठ कर,
ठेकरियाँ पानी की सतह पे फेंकता रहा
घोड़े देखता था दौड़ते हुए

सर्दी से ठिठरने लगता था कभी
छद्री छद्री धूप ओढ़ लेता था

कल सुना है बर्फ़ गिर रही थी जब पहाड़ों पर
खिड़की खोल कर . . .
वो आग तापने चला गया . . . चिता की आग पर!

Jagjit Singh: An Elegy

A strange chill had arrived
And settled like a lump in his heart
He would set alight a *kangri* of ghazals and warm himself

When he returned after lighting his son's pyre
He skipped stones across the water
Watched them like horses running.

He would start to shiver in the cold
And shroud himself in sunlight.

I heard that when the snow fell yesterday on the mountains
He opened his window and went to warm himself
On the fire of a burning pyre.

महदी हसन

आँखों को वीज़ा नहीं लगता!

आँखों को वीज़ा नहीं लगता
सपनों की सरहद होती नहीं
बंद आँखों से रोज़ मैं सरहद पार चला जाता हूँ,
मिलने 'महदी हसन' से!

सुनता हूँ उनकी आवाज़ को चोट लगी है
और ग़ज़ल ख़ामोश है सामने बैठी हुई
काँप रहे हैं होंट ग़ज़ल के
जब कहते हैं . . .
'सूख गये हैं फूल किताबों में
यार "फ़राज़" भी बिछड़ गये हैं, अब शायद मिलें वो ख़्वाब में!'
बंद आँखों से अक्सर सरहद पार चला जाता हूँ मैं!

आँखों को वीज़ा नहीं लगता
सपनों की सरहद, कोई नहीं!

Mehdi Hassan

EYES DON'T NEED A VISA

Eyes don't require a visa
Dreams have no borders
With eyes closed, I cross the border every day
To meet Mehdi Hassan.

I've learnt his voice has suffered hurt
And facing him, the ghazal sits silent
With lips atremble
When he says,
'The flowers have dried inside the books
Friend 'Faraz' has also left now, perhaps to meet in dreams only.'
Through closed eyes, often I cross the border.

Eyes don't require a visa
Dreams have no borders.

सलिल चौधरी (जिनियस)

सलिलदा सच मुच एक जिनियस थे। और एक ऐसा जिनियस जो ख़ुद उनके क़ाबू में नहीं रहता था। मैंने उन्हें तर्ज़ बनाने में कभी effort करते हुए नहीं देखा। जब बैठे पियानो पर, या हार्मोनियम पर फ़ौरन एक तर्ज़ तैयार कर लेते थे, पर बैठते ज़रा मुश्किल से थे। धुन बनाते बनाते ही बँगला में गीत भी लिख लेते थे। शायर, कहानीकार, पेंटर और डायरेक्शन भी की . . . 'पिंजरे के पँछी'। बँगला और उर्दू में उनके साथ बहुत सी नज़्में बाँटीं।

लेकिन उस आज़ाद जिनियस को क़ाबू करना नामुमकिन था। पतला दुबला सा जिस्म अपनी ही शिद्दत से काँपता रहता था। शिद्दत मतलब intensity।

सलिल चौधरी

कपकपाती हुई तालाब के पानी की सतह
सूत के तागा से बाँधे हुए सैलाब का शोर
हलकी सी ज़र्ब से झन्नाके बज उठते हैं
तेज़ चाकू के तराशे हुए चेहरे के नक़ूश
मुज़तरब चेहरे पे उड़ते हुए आँखों के हुरूफ़
इक तजस्सुस में हैं, लगता है किसी पल भी
अपने ही सफ़हे से घबरा के ये उड़ जायेंगे

अपने ही आपसे घबरा के न छुट जाये कहीं
ख़ुद से उलझी हुई ऐसी परवाज़!

Salil Chowdhury (A Genius)

Salil Da was really a true genius. A genius spirit that was beyond his own control. I have never seen him having to make an effort while creating a tune. Whenever he sat at the piano or harmonium, a tune would immediately present itself to him. But he would shirk from applying himself to the task. He would craft lyrics in Bangla while composing his tunes. Poet, storyteller, painter . . . he was a director too, of *Pinjre ki Panchi*. We shared many a poem in both Bangla and Urdu.

But it was impossible for him to hold in that free-spirited genius, the intensity of which would create a constant tremour in his thin frame.

Salil Chowdhury: A Portrait

Like the water that stands trembling in the pond
The flood of music that had been bound by threads of yarn
Would, at the slightest touch, start to resound
Engraved as with a sharp knife, the features of his face.
The fluttering eyes on the restless visage
It looks as if at any moment
Will fly away from its page.

A flight that it may take, disturbed by its own urge.

कानू रॉय

एक ग़रीब मौसीक़ार था। बासू की सब फ़िल्मों में उसके साथ गाने लिक्खे। सिवाय आख़री फ़िल्म 'आस्था' के। जब तक वो जा चुका था। 'हावड़ा पुल' पर वेल्डर का काम किया था। 'डगा' गोद में लेकर पुल पार कर गया।

कानू रॉय

जीते जी, इक मौसीक़ी की धुन चलती रहती है
आरकेस्ट्रा है, इक सिंफ़नी है
सांस का सुर, और धड़कन की लय चलती रहती है

कानू था नां—'कानू रॉय'
गोद में 'डगा' रखके, तिती तिती कर के गाता था

बजते बजते ही सब 'डगा' ऐसे 'सम' पे पड़ा कि फिर आवाज़ न निकली
ख़ामोश हुआ
वो फुल स्टोप था
यूँ मौत हुई!

Kanu Roy

He was an impoverished musician. Working with Basu, he composed all the songs for Basu's films. Except for the last film *Aastha*. Because he was gone by then.

He used to work as a welder on the Howrah Bridge. Holding his 'daga' on his lap, he crossed the bridge.

Kanu Roy

All through life, a musician's tunes continue to resound
Orchestrated, like a symphony
The music of breath, the heartbeat's rhythm
Play on.

Kanu, you know . . . 'Kanu Roy'
He would keep the 'daga' on his lap
And sing ti ti ti ti to set his tunes.

Even as it kept playing, the 'daga' reached the 'sum'
In such a way
That it fell silent. No sound emerged.
Only silence.
That is how death came!!
It was a full stop!!

पँचम

जिसकी शख़्सियत पर पूरी किताब लिख सकता हूँ, उसे चार जुमलों में बयान नहीं कर सकता।
जितना भी कहूँगा, वो कम रहेगा।

रौशनी है तो सही, कम कम है
आँख शायद मेरी, फिर से नम है
यूँ नहीं बनते सुरीले रिश्ते
सात सुर लगते हैं इक पँचम है!

पँचम

याद है, बारिशों का दिन पँचम
जब पहाड़ी के नीचे वादी में
धुंद से झांक कर निकलती हुई
रेल की पटरीयाँ गुज़रती थीं

धुंद में ऐसे लग रहे थे हम
जैसे दो पौधे पास बैठे हों
हम बहुत देर तक वहाँ बैठे
उस मुसाफ़िर का ज़िक्र करते रहे
जिसको आना था पिछली शब, लेकिन
जिसकी आमद का वक़्त टलता रहा

Pancham

I cannot describe in four sentences, the personality on whom I could write an entire book. However much I may write, it will not suffice.

There is light, but it glimmers low
Perhaps because my eyes are ready to flow
Musical relationships are not created thus
There are seven notes, and one is Pancham.

Pancham

Do you remember that rainy day, Pancham
When in the valley below the mountains
Peeping through the gentle mists
The train tracks would go past.

In the hazy mist we looked
Like two plants sitting close together
Long we would stay, sitting there
Talking about that traveller
Who was to arrive last evening, but
Whose arrival was being constantly delayed.

देर तक पट्रीयों पे बैठे हुए
ट्रेन का इंतेज़ार करते रहे
ट्रेन आई, न उसका वक़्त हुआ
और तुम यूँही दो क़दम चल कर
धुंद पर पाँव रखके चल भी दिये
मैं अकेला हूँ धुंद में पँचम!

Long we sat along the train tracks
Waiting for the train to come
Neither the train, nor the time for it did come
And you, taking two steps, stepping into the mist
Left.
I am alone sitting in the mist, Pancham.

चिराग़ पँचम (म्युज़िक सिटिंग)

सुलगती है अभी सिग्रेट तुम्हारी उंगलियों में,
'पँचम'!
तलब है होंटों पर, आँखों में आमद है

थिरकने लग गये हैं हाथ 'मारूती' के तबले पर,
'मनोहर' भी लिप्टता जा रहा है बाँसुरी में
तुम्हारी धुन पे साज़ सुर चढ़ने लगे हैं

'चिराग़' सो भी चुका है आँख बँद कर के
धुआँ अब तक ख़ला में गुनगुनाता है!

उतरो आओ आँखों से काग़ज़ पर
तुम्हारी धुन पे कुछ अल्फ़ाज़ रख दूँ!

Chiragh (Music Sitting)

The cigarette still smoulders between your fingers,
Pancham!
The desire to sing is on your lips; the inspiration in your eyes.

Maruti's fingers have started dribbling on the tabla
Manohari too is getting wrapped up in the flute
Instruments and notes have started to embellish your humming.

'Chiragh' has closed his eyes and sunk into sleep,
The smoke still hums softly in the void.

Come down, descend
So I may place down on paper
Some words for your tune.

आशा भोंसले

आशा भोंसले . . . इतनी बड़ी legend हैं हमारे दौर की, लेकिन कभी लेजेंड की तरह पेश नहीं आईं। अपने हाथ से पकाया भी, परोसा भी, खिलाया भी। इंतेज़ार करते थे, कब बेकग्राऊँड म्युज़िक में रात की शिफ़्ट (shift) आये और उनके हाथ से पका गोश्त खायें। पँचम के रिश्ते से उन्हें 'बौदी' ही बुलाता हूँ।

ज़िंदगी में उतार-चढ़ाव भी बहुत देखे। घर घराने भी बदले। बड़ी ज़िंदा दिली से जीती हैं।

आशा बौदी

इक छींटा है अश्कों का
और धूप का झोंका है
उस जिस्म की मिट्टी में
वो पौधा सुरों का है

आवाज़ टहनी पर
अल्फ़ाज़ कहीं रख दो
होंटों की तरह उनके
मानी खिल उठते हैं

Asha Bhosle

Asha Bhosle . . . such a legend of our times; but she has never presented herself as one. She has cooked for us herself, served us, fed us. How impatiently we would wait, hoping for the recording sessions of background music to begin so that, during the night shift, we would get to taste the mutton she cooks so well. I address her as 'Boudi' because of my relationship with Pancham.

She has seen the ups and downs of life. Changed homes as destiny dictated. She lives life to the full, with total commitment.

Asha Boudi

A sprinkling of tears, a burst of sunshine
From the body of that clay
A sapling of musical notes.

Place the words anywhere
On a branch of her voice
And their meaning
Flowers, full blown,
On her lips.

देखा है, मगर अक्सर
मौसम जब कवर्ट ले
और तेज़ हवा हो तो,
लटका हुआ शाख़ों पर
इक घोंसला हिलता है

किस 'ठाठ' से गूँधा था?
है नीम की ठँडक भी
और सूरज का झोंका भी
वो पौधा सुरों का है!

Yet, often when the weather shifts
And harsh winds blow
As it hangs precariously from a branch
A nest trembles.

Which 'thaat' was kneaded thus?
Holding in it the cool of the neem
This burst of sunshine . . .
A sapling of melodious notes.

मीना

किसी के जाने पर कैसे गिला करे कोई
बड़ी क़रीब से उठ कर चला गया कोई

मीना

आँखें बँद कर के सो गयी
और मर गयी!
उसके बाद उसने साँस भी न ली!
एक लँबी हादसात से भरी
पेचदार ज़िंदगी के बाद,
कितनी सीधी और सहल सी मौत थी!

Meena

How can one complain when someone leaves
Someone very close, just got up and went away.

Meena

Shutting her eyes, she fell asleep
And died.
Did not even take a breath afterwards
After a long, eventful life
Filled with torturous trials
How simple and easy her death!

अमजद ख़ान

माई डियर हिज़ हेवीनीस।

अमजद भाई में एक शहाना बात थी। अदब आदाब और सलीक़े में बादशाह लगते थे। इंडस्ट्री में जुनियर आर्टिस्ट जिन्हें लोग 'ऐक्सट्रा' कह देते हैं, उनकी यूनियन के लिये बहुत काम किया अमजद भाई ने।

सच में वो दोस्त दिल का शहंशाह था—कल चला गया . . .

अमजद ख़ान

वो दोस्त कल गुज़र गया
वो दोस्त अब नहीं रहा
ग़रुब-ए-आफ़ताब के
सुन्हेरी पेड़ के तले
जहाँ वो रोज़ मिलता था
वहीं पे दफ़्न कर दिया

मैं नीम अँधेरी क़ब्र में
सुला रहा था जब उसे
तो नीम-व-निगाह से
वो देखता रहा मुझे

Amjad Khan

My dear, His Heaviness!

There was something regal about Amjad Bhai. His courtesies, mannerisms and communications carried the aura of royalty. For those junior artistes in the industry whom others dismiss as 'extras', and for their Union, Amjad Bhai gave a lot of support.

Verily, this friend was an emperor at heart.

He went away yesterday.

Amjad Khan

That friend died yesterday
He does not exist any more
Under the golden tree
Of the setting sun
Where we would meet every day
We buried him just there.

As I laid him to rest
In the semi-darkness of his grave
He continued to look at me
With half-opened eyes.

हतेलियों से आँख के
चिराग़ भी बुझा दिये
कि दो जहाँ के सिलसिले
ज़मीं पे ही चुका दिये

मैं जब वहाँ से लौटा तो
वो साथ साथ आ गया
वो दोस्त जो नहीं रहा
जो दोस्त कल गुज़र गया!

With my palms I put out
The light of his eyes
So the connections across two worlds
Were repaid on earth itself.

When I returned from there
He came along with me
The friend who passed away
The friend who died yesterday.

संजीव कुमार

जवानी में उससे अच्छा बूढ़ा एक्टर नहीं देखा। २३ साल के थे, जब (Ibsen) इब्सन के प्ले 'All My Sons' में बाप का रोल करते थे। लीला चिटनिस उनकी बीवी बनती थीं।

फ़िल्मों में आने से बहुत पहले, वहीं 'हरी' से मुलाक़ात हुई थी। चवन्नी, अट्ठनी का उधार आपस में चलता रहता था। जैसे ही कमाई अच्छी हुई, तो मुझे हुक्म था कि 'घर में एक बोतल "ब्लैक लेबल" की हमेशा रखना, मैं रात को कभी भी धमक सकता हूँ।' उसके लिये non-veg भी बना के रखना पड़ता था, क्योंकि उसके अपने घर में नहीं पक सकता था। संजीव के साथ बड़ा याराना था।

एक दूसरे को वो सब कह लेते थे, जो कोई दूसरा नहीं कह सकता। मेरा पान खाना छुड़ा दिया था उसने। मैं अब तक नहीं खाता। चाहे तो आके देखले!

संजीव कुमार

'हैली कोमेट' की तरह गुज़रा है जो साल,
अभी . . . गुज़रा नहीं
देर तक तैरेगा बर्फ़ाब धुआँ सा इसका
देर तक गर्द उड़ायेगा ज़मीं की छत पर!

वो जो 'संजीव' गया है नां, अभी पास से उठकर
उसकी साँसें मेरे पहलू में अभी तैर रही हैं
मेरी दीवार पे उसकी पीठ का ख़म बाक़ी है अब तक
सिर्फ़ तारीख़ ही बदली है, सफ़हा बदला नहीं!

Sanjeev Kumar

In his youth, there was no better 'old' actor than him. He was twenty-three when he played the role of the father in Ibsen's *All My Sons*. Leela Chitnis played his wife.

I met Hari there, long before he joined the films. We would borrow petty change from each other. As soon as my earnings improved, his diktat to me was 'Always keep a bottle of "Black Label" in your house. I can drop in at night, any day.' I had to keep non-veg dishes also ready for him, as meat was not cooked in his house. Sanjeev and I were close friends. We could tell each other things we could never tell anyone else. He stopped my paan eating habit. I still do not have paan. If he wishes, he can come and check.

Sanjeev Kumar

The year that zoomed past like Hailey's Comet . . .
Is not yet gone
Its cold smoke will rise for a long time yet
And for a long time blow dust on earth's roof.

That Sanjeev, who just got up from beside me and left
His breath still floats around me.
The curve of his back remains etched on my wall.
Only the date has changed, the page has not been turned.

ओम पूरी

सुबह चाय के साथ 'रस्क' (टोस्ट) खाना उसका दिलपसंद नियम था। घर पे भी, बाहर भी!

मेरे घर के आस पास से भी गुज़र जाये तो चाय के साथ 'रस्क' खाने ज़रूर आ जाता था। मेरे लिये लाज़िम हो गया था, घर में 'रस्क' रखना।

अच्छे 'रस्क' रखने के लिये अच्छी बेकरी की तलाश हमेशा रहती थी। ओम नयी नयी बेकरियों की ख़बर लाया करता था।

उसने अपने लिये तो एक मुस्तक़िल बेकरी ढूँड ली। अब मुझे अपने लिये एक बेकरी तलाश करनी होगी!

ओम पूरी

कभी देखा है कैसे बेकरी में
डबल रोटी का आटा भर के साँचों में
दहकती भट्टी में लुढ़का के ट्रोली पर
अचानक बँद कर देते हैं दरवाज़ा
के पक जाये !

Om Puri

He was in the habit of having rusk with his tea. Whether at home or elsewhere. Even if he was just passing by in the vicinity of my house, he would definitely drop in to have tea and rusk. Thus, it became necessary for me to keep rusks at home.

He was always in search of good bakeries that would supply good quality rusks. Om would bring me information about new bakeries on every visit.

He has found a permanent bakery for himself. I need to look for a bakery for myself now.

Om Puri

Have you ever seen
How, filling the bread dough into a mould
They flip it on to the trolley
Inside a blazing oven
And instantly slam the door shut
To cook it.

उसे कल ले गये थे ट्रोली पर रख कर
उसे लुढ़का के बिजली से दहकती भट्टी के अँदर
और फ़ौरन बँद कर डाला था दरवाज़ा
कि पक जाये!

पका के क्या मिलेगा?
ख़ाक!

We took him yesterday, on a trolley
And placing him in the blazing electric oven
Immediately closed the door
So that he'd be cooked.

What will come of that cooking?
Ashes!

अंजना भाभी

जगत भाभी थी, ये अंजना भाभी, प्रोड्युसर, डारेक्टर, 'एच.एस.रवेल' की पत्नी। घर में हमेशा महमानों की चहल पहल लगी रहती थी। लोगों के मसले हल करती रहती थीं, और रिश्ते कराती रहती थीं। लेकिन बड़ी बात थी बँगाली लिट्रेचर से लब्रेज़ और पँजाबी लोक गीतों का भँडार थीं। कोई पँजाबी कह नहीं सकता था के वो बँगालन हैं। और कोई बँगाली उन्हें सुन कर पँजाबन नहीं कह सकता था। सब की दोस्त . . . सब की भाभी!

एक दिन पता नहीं क्या हुआ—ढेर सारी नींद की गोलियाँ खा लीं . . . और सो गयीं।

ईंधन

छोटे थे, माँ उपले थापा करती थीं
हम उपलों पर शक्लें गूँधा करते थे
आँख लगा कर—कान बना कर
नाक सजा कर—
पगड़ी वाला, टोपी वाला
मेरा उपला, तेरा उपला
अपने अपने जाने पहचाने नामों से
उपले थापा करते थे

Anjana Bhabhi

She was Bhabhi to all in the world, our Anjana Bhabhi . . . producer, director S.H. Rawail's wife. Her house was always filled with the chatter of guests. She was eternally solving people's problems. And fixing marriages. The amazing thing about her was that she was a storehouse of Bengali literature and a font of Punjabi folk songs. No Punjabi would ever say that she was from Bengal. And no Bengali who heard her speak would say she was a Punjaban. Everybody's friend . . . everyone's Bhabi.

Don't know what happened . . . one day, she took a whole lot of sleeping pills and went to sleep.

Indhan

When we were kids, Mother would make dung cakes
And we would knead faces on them
Make eyes—Fix ears
Shape a nose
Pagree wallah, topi wallah,
my *upla*—your upla
Using names familiar to each of us
We would brand the cakes.

हँस्ता खेलता सूरज रोज़ सवेरे आकर
गोबर के उपलों पे खेला करता था

रात को आँगन में जब चुल्हा जलता था
हम सब उसको घेर के बैठे रहते थे
किस उपले की बारी आई
किसका उपला राख हुआ
वो पंडित था—
इक मुन्ना था—
इक दशरथ था—

बरसों बाद—
शमशान में बैठा सोच रहा हूँ
आज की रात इस वक़्त के जलते चुल्हे में
इक दोस्त का उपला और गया!

The playful, laughing sun would every morning
Play about on the cakes of dung

When the oven in the courtyard was lit at night
We would sit surrounding it
Whose upla's turn would it be
Whose upla had turned to ashes
That was a pandit
And that, Munna
And this, Dasharath . . .

Years later, I sit
In the cremation ground thinking
This night, in time's burning oven
Another friend's upla has been burnt.

मेराज

मेरे अस्सिटेंट थे—

बहुत ख़ुशख़त लिखते थे। मेरी स्क्रिप्ट फ़ैर करते थे, फिर डायरेक्शन में अस्सिटेंट हो गये।

इलाहबाद के पास एक गाँव से थे, और हमेशा गाँव ही के रहे। शहर उन्हें रास नहीं आया। शहर में हमेशा बेचैन रहते थे। शादी भी करली। फ़िल्में भी डायरेक्ट कीं। लेकिन गाँव की मिट्टी हमेशा खींचती रही उन्हें . . . और आख़िरकार वहीं जाकर मिट्टी पहन ली!

मेराज: पोटरेट

काग़ज़ी हैं पैरहन!
कोई लिबादा रूह का ऐसे नहीं? . . .
जो मुस्तक़िल हो!
वो, जिसे न आग झुलसे
वो, जो पानी में गले, न जिसके लिखे नक़्श पिघलें
धूप छाँव और हवा जिस पर असर अँदाज़ न हो
जिस्म के पैकर, जो रूहों ने पहन रखे हैं फ़ानी हैं
'वासांसी जीर्णि यथा विहाय . . . '
कग़ज़ी है पैरहन
हर पैकरे तस्वीर का!

Meraj

He was my assistant. He would write the fair versions of my scripts, and later was an assistant in direction too. He belonged to a village near Allahabad. And remained a villager at heart. The city did not appeal to him. He was always restless here. He married. Directed a film too. But the soil of his village continued to tug at his heart . . . and finally, that's where he went to wrap himself in its soil.

Meraj: A Portrait

Life is transient . . .
The spirit wears no robe
That is permanent.
One, that no fire can scorch,
Or water melt away, nor his features erode
On which neither the sun, nor shade, nor the wind
Has any influence
The appearance of body that the spirit wears is temporal
'Vasamsi Jarnani Yatha Vihaya'
Life is transient . . .
The spirit wears no robe

मेराज

जिस्म हमेशा ही से एक वबाले जाँ था !
आग झुलस देती है
बर्फ़ से गल जाता है
पेट की ख़ातिर, हड्डियाँ तोड़नी पड़ती हैं
बोझ उठा कर, ऊँचे कोहसारों पे चढ़ना
कोहनियाँ, कँधे छिल जाते हैं . . .
तुँद हवायें, जिस्म की दीवारों को छेदने लगती हैं

जिस्म हमेशा ही से एक वबाले जाँ था
ख़स्ता सा बस एक मकाँ था
कितने साल भला मिट्टी के कच्चे एक मकाँ में रहते !

Meraj

The body has always been a source of trouble
Fire could scorch it
Ice would melt it
One has to break one's bones to feed the stomach
Carry weights up mountainous slopes
Causing elbows and shoulders to blister
While icy winds drill through the body's walls.

The body has always been a source of trouble
Just a perishable dwelling
How many years can one live in a perishable house made of mud?

विशाल—वो मौसीक़ार है . . .!

वो मौसीक़ार है, इक धुन मुझे दे कर गया है
कि मैं अल्फ़ाज़ से गिरहें लगा कर बाँध दूं उसको
कहीं वो बह न जाये!

वो दिन भर गूँजती रहती है धुन, सर में
कोई भँवरा सा मँडलाता है जो बेचैन रखता है
कली फूटे कोई अब ज़हन में तो
किसी मिसरे पे भँवरा बैठ जाये!

Vishal—He's a Musician!

He's a composer, he's left a tune with me
So that, knotting it up in words, I can tie it down
So it won't float away.

All day, through the day, the tune resounds in my head
Humming like a bee, making me restless
If only a flower could burst open in my mind, then
The bee could settle on the lines of the song.

रेखा भारद्वाज

एक और नाम भी है इस लड़की का—अज़ीज़ा! और उसी नाम से उसने साज़िन्दों की अपनी एक टोली बना रक्खी है, जिसे अँग्रेज़ी में बैंड कहते हैं।

एक सूफ़ियाना मिज़ाज है रेखा में। उसे अंथक ताक़त देता है, महेनत की और रीयाज़ की। वो कहीं पहुँचना चाहती है। और ख़ुद को पा लेने की कोशिश में लगी रहती है—और कभी कभी थक भी जाती है। मैंने एक बार सुन लिया था . . .

एक नदी की बात सुनी . . .

एक नदी की बात सुनी
इक शायर से पूछ रही थी
रोज़ किनारे दोनों हाथ पकड़ के मेरे
सीधी राह चलाते हैं
रोज़ ही तो मैं
नाव भर कर, पीठ पे लेकर
कितने लोग हैं पार उतार के आती है

रोज़ मेरे सीने पे लहरे
नाबालिग़ बच्चों के जैसे
कुछ कुछ लिखती रहती हैं

Rekha Bhardwaj

This girl has yet another name . . . Azeeza. And this is the name she has created for a group of musical-minded people; in English it could be called a band. There is a mystical side to Rekha. Which gives her the inner strength for perseverance and practice. She wants to achieve something, get somewhere. And strives to find her inner self. Sometimes, it tires her out.

I happened to hear it once, she was asking . . .

I Listened to a River Talking . . .

I listened to a river talking
She was asking a poet
Every day the shores, holding both my hands
Walk me down straight paths
Every day I fill countless people into boats
And carrying them across on my back
Return after setting them safely across.

Every day the waves
Like a child, keep writing something or the other
On my bosom.

क्या ऐसा हो सकता है जब
कुछ भी न हो
कुछ भी नहीं . . .
और अपनी तह से पीठ लगा के इक शब रुकी रहूँ
बस ठहरी रहूँ
जैसे कविता कह लेने के बाद पड़ी रह जाती है
मैं पड़ी रहूँ!

Can it ever happen that
When there is nothing
Simply nothing
I curl myself up and stop for an entire night
Just stay still
Just like a poem lies quiet once recited
I just lie still.

III

बिरजू महाराज

पाठ शाला ऐसी लुभावनी होती है। और ऐसी सुरीली, ये बात बिरजू महाराज के पास बैठ कर ही पता चलता है। उनके पास बैठ जाओ तो संगीत की सिक्षा ही सिक्षा बिछ जाती है।

एक ज़माने में मुझे उनके चचा लच्छू महाराज की सेवा का मौक़ा भी मिला था।

कथक की महीन कारियाँ, बँदिशें और भाव। जब भी बैठा हूँ बिरजू महाराज के पास, झोली भर के ही लौटा हूँ। दिनों तक आँखों और कान गूँजते रहते हैं!

बिरजू महाराज

आपने देखा था क्या?
वक़्त उतरा था फ़लक से जब
पाँव में घुँघरू थे उसके!
लय ही लय, ताल ही ताल
एक उड़ती हुई घुरनी . . .
वक़्त के पेट से निकला हुआ एक बगोला

बोल यूँ गूँजते हैं जैसे
कोई पीतल के बने लफ़्ज़ों को तोड़ रहा है

Birju Maharaj

So, a school can be beguiling too! And so very tuneful! This truth can only be known by sitting with Birju Maharaj. He spreads a garden filled with melodious lesson after lesson on music for those who sit beside him.

Once, long ago, I found a chance to be of service to his uncle, Lachchu Maharaj too.

Kathak's intricate pathways, *bandishes* and musical texts, its emotions . . . after each visit with Birju Maharaj, I would return laden with these gifts of knowledge. And for days after, the sights would occupy my mind, the music resound in my ears.

Birju Maharaj

Have you seen how
When Time descended from the skies
He came wearing bells on his feet!
Laden with musical notes
Rich with rhythm
A whirlwind born out of Time's core.

The *bols* resound as if
Breaking asunder syllables of brass.

हमने तो सूरज को जब उठते हुए देखा था, उफ़क़ से
कह के 'ता थैया' उठा था
किरनें लड़ियों की तरह छूट के बिखरी थीं ज़मीं पर
पृथ्वी गूँज उठी थी

वक़्त की लय को पहन रखा है पाँव में किसने?
घड़ियाँ चलती हैं तो पैरों की धमक,
कानों में पड़ती है, ता थई . . .
ता थई, ता ता थई . . . ता ता थई!

When we saw the sun rising on the horizon
He said *taa thaiya* as he rose
Strands of sunlight scattered across the soil
The earth echoed with sound.

Who has worn the rhythms of time on his feet?
When the clocks tick, the striking of feet
Reaches our ears . . . *ta thei,*
Ta thei . . . ta ta thei . . .!

पंडित हरिप्रसाद चौरसिया

एक गीत लिखा था, लकड़ी की बांसुरी पर। और कोई एक फूँक से उस बांसुरी में जान डाल सकता है, ये सिर्फ़ हरिप्रसाद चौरसिया को सुन कर महसूस हुआ। ये नज़्म या गीत कहिये, मैं उन्हीं के नाम मनसूब करना चाहता हूँ ! इतने साल एक साथ काम किया। पता नहीं था इतने बड़े legend के साथ रहा मैं !

बंसी

सातों बार बोले बंसी
एक ही बार बोले ना
तन की लागी सारी बोले
मन की लागी खोले ना . . .

चुपके सुर में भेद छुपाये
फूँक-फूँक बतलाये
तन की सीधी मन की घुन्नी
पच्चीस पेंचे खाये

प्रीत की पीड़ा जाने मुई
छाती छेद पड़े
उठ-उठ के फिर मुँह लगती है
कान्हा संग लड़े

Pandit Hariprasad Chaurasia

I had written a song about a bamboo *bansi*. That someone could bring a reed alive with one puff of breath, I realized only when I heard Hariprasad Chaurasia. I wish to dedicate this song, or you could call it a poem, to him. For years I worked with him, unaware I was working with such a legend.

Bansi

Seven notes the bansi reveals
Even as she conceals one
Sings of all that touches her body
Won't reveal that which touches her heart.

Tucks away her mysteries in her silence
Releases them in puffs of breath
Straight of body, artful of mind
Restlessly twists and turns.

Love's agonies she well knows,
Heart pierced like a sieve
Yet rising time and again touches Krishna's lips
To pick a quarrel with him.

हाँ बोले, ना बोले, बोले ना
तन की लागी सारी बोले,
मन की लागी खोले ना . . .

Says yes, says no, says nothing at all
Sings of all that touches her body
Won't reveal that which touches her heart.

गोपीचंद नारंग

आपकी पैदाइश 'बलोचिस्तान' में हुई। प्रोफ़ेसर हैं। हमारे दौर में, उर्दू के बड़े नक़्क़ाद और दानिशवर हैं। उर्दू की ख़िदमात के लिये, पाकिस्तान का सब से बड़ा ख़िताब 'सितारा इमतियाज़' हासिल कर चुके हैं। और हिंदुस्तान में 'पद्म भूषण'!

गोपीचंद नारंग: पोटरेट

दो पहूहियों पे चलता दरया
इक पाँव पे ठहरी झील
झील की नाभी पर रक्खी है
उर्दू की रौशन क़न्दील
रौशनी जब भँवराती है तो
झील भँवर बन जाती है

भँवर भँवर, और
महवर महवर, इल्म का साग़र छलक रहा है
तशन-ए-लब सब ओक लगाये देख रहे हैं
छलकेगा तो नूर गिरेगा, नूर पियेंगे!

Gopichand Narang

Born in Balochisthan, he is a professor; Recognized far and wide as a learned and eminent authority on Urdu. In acknowledgment of his huge contribution to Urdu, he has been conferred with Pakistan's highest honour, 'Sitara Imtiaz'. While India has honoured him with the Padma Bhushan award.

Gopichand Narang: A Portrait

The river runs swift on two nimble feet
The lake stands silent on one
And in the lake's navel is placed
The bright light of Urdu's candle
When the candle spreads its light
The lake becomes a whirlpool.

In whirlpool after whirlpool, axis after axis
The spring of knowledge sparkles
In an attitude of thirst, with palm cupped
They are watching
It will overflow; atoms of light will fall
They will drink of it.

मुंशी प्रेमचंद

हमेशा अपने ही क़स्बे गाँव और मोहल्ले के राईटर लगते हैं। कुछ रिश्तेदार जैसे लगते हैं। उनकी कहानियाँ, नोवेल (novel) पढ़ते हुए महसूस होता है, उन्हें देखा है। वो जो नुक्कड़ पे बैठे, अख़बार घुटनों पर, चश्मा नाक से फिसला हुआ, और आस पास के गाँव की ख़बरें सुना रहे हैं।

मैं कई बार मिला उनसे। पहले पहल स्कूल में जब 'ईदगाह' सुनी थी . . . फिर कॉलेज में मिला और दूसरी कहानियाँ सुनी और 'गोदान' पढ़ा। वही कहानियाँ थी, पर उनकी गहराई हर बार बढ़ती चली गयी।

फिर जब और बड़ा हुआ, तो वही कहानियाँ दूसरों को सुनाना शुरू कीं।

शहर आकर लोग उन्हें भूल जाते हैं। इसी लिये उनसे मिलने के लिये, अपनी जड़ों पर वापस जाना पड़ता है।

'प्रेमचंद की सोहबत तो अच्छी लगती है
लेकिन उनकी सोहबत में तकलीफ़ बहुत है!'

मुंशी प्रेमचंद

प्रेमचंद की सोहबत तो अच्छी लगती है
लेकिन उनकी सोहबत में तकलीफ़ बहुत है!

Munshi Premchand

He has always been the chronicler of towns, villages and localities. As if he's part of the family. Reading his stories and novels gives the feeling that he is a familiar figure, someone you might know. Sitting at the street corner, a newspaper on his knees, spectacles slipping down his nose as he reads out the news about nearby villages loudly to all.

I have met him many times. First, in school when I listened to 'Idgah' . . . then I met him in college and listened to other stories by him, and read 'Godan'. They were the same stories but with every reading, they acquired new depths of meaning.

As I grew older, I started narrating the stories to others.

People who come to the cities forget him. Which is why, to meet him, it is necessary to return to one's roots.

'Meeting Premchand is indeed pleasant
But being in his company is also agonizing.'

Munshi Premchand

Meeting Premchand is indeed pleasant
But being in his company is also agonizing

मुंशी जी . . .
आपने कितने दर्द दिये हैं
हमको भी, और जिनको आपने पीस पीस के मारा है

'होरी' का पिस्ते रहना और एक सदी तक
पोर पोर दिखलाते रहे हो
किस गाय की पूँछ पकड़ के बैंकुठ पार कराना था?
सड़क किनारे, पत्थर कूटते जान गँवा दी, और सड़क न पार हुई,
या तुमने करवायी नहीं?

धनिया बच्चे जन्ती, पालती, अपने और पराये भी
ख़ाली गोद रही आख़िर में
कहती रही वो . . .
डूबना है तो, बोल गढ़ई क्या? गँगा क्या?

हामिद की दादी चूल्हे पर बैठी हाथ जलाती रही
कितनी देर लगायी तुमने, इक चिमटा पकड़ाने में?

घेसू ने भी कूज़ा कूज़ा, उम्र की सारी बोतल पी ली
तिलछट चाट के आख़िर उसकी बुध्दी फूटी
नंगे जी सकते हैं तो फिर, बिना कफ़न जलने में क्या है?

Munshi ji . . .
You have inflicted so much pain
On me too, and on those whom you have mercilessly beaten.
For an entire century you have been showing us
The myriad ways Hori has been tormented and tortured
Holding which cow by the tail, did he hope to cross heaven's gates?
He lost his life breaking stones along the road
Never once crossing to the other side
Nor did you help him across.

'Dhaniya' birthed children, tended them,
Her own and those of others too
Yet, in the end her lap remained empty
If one has to drown, she kept saying
Ditch or Ganga, does it matter?

Hamid's grandmother burnt her hands
At the kitchen fire every day
How long it took for you
To hand her a pair of tongs!

Gheesu too, drank bottle after bottle of life's bitters
Wisdom dawned only after he touched the bottom
If one can live in nakedness, what is wrong
In burning a body without a shroud?

एक सेर, एक पाव गंदुम,
दाना दाना सूद चुकाते
सांस की गिन्ती छूट गयी . . .
तीन तीन पुश्तों को बँध्वा मज़दूरी में बाँध के
तुमने क़लम उठाली . . .
शंकर महत्व की नसलें अब तक वो सूद चुकाती हैं!

ठाकुर का कुआँ, और ठाकुर के कुएँ से, इक लोटा पानी के लिये
दिल के सूते सूख गये!
झोकू के जिस्म में एक बार फिर 'रीदास' को मारा तुमने!

मुंशी जी . . .
आप विधाता तो न थे पर
लेखक थे अपने किर्दारों की क़िस्मत तो लिख सकते थे!

One *ser*, one pav of wheat
Paying off debts grain by grain
They have lost count of their breath
Imprisoning three generations in bonded labour
You put down your pen . . .
Generations of Shankar Mahto's progeny
Are still paying back what he borrowed.

The well of the high caste thakur . . .
Awaiting a lota of water from the thakur's well
The sinews of the heart went dry
Once again, you flayed saint Raidas
In Jhoku's bare body.

Munshiji . . .
You were not the Creator, but
A writer you certainly were; and could have rewritten
The destinies of your characters.

जतिन दास

हिंदुस्तान के बड़े नामोर पेंटर हैं।

हमेशा एक एनर्जी से भरे हुए मिलते हैं। उड़ीसा में उनके नाम की एक फ़ाईन आर्ट एकेडमी भी है।

'चाँद पुखराज' का नाम से मेरा एक नज़्मों का मजमुआ शाय हुआ था, जिसके लिये उन्होंने अपने स्केचज़ (sketches) से नवाज़ा था।

जतिन दास

एक मुसव्विर,
हाथ उठा कर,
चाँद के चाक से फिर आकाश पे गर्म लकीरें खींच रहा है

पैलेट (palette) के ऊपर रक्खी है गर्म शफ़क़
लिपटाता है, खोलता है, आकाश का कैनवास
उँगलियों से लिपटी हुई है
कुछ नौ-ज़ायेदा जिस्मों की गीली मिट्टी

जिस्मों के कूज़ों पे झुक कर
सूरज के क़तरे टपका के,
चेहरों के नुसख़े लिखता है
साँसें लेती आँखें उनके ऊपर रखके,
ढूँढता है
इन चेहरों में कौन-सा चेहरा उसका है!

Jatin Das

He is one of India's renowned painters. Always carries with him a bristling energy whenever we meet. There's a Fine Art academy in Odisa, named after him. I had published a collection of my poems, titled 'Chand Pukhraj Ka'. He embellished it with his sketches.

Jatin Das

A painter
Raised his arm
And using the moon as chalk
Drew burning lines on the sky.

The twilight burns on his palette
He folds, unfolds, the sky's canvas
Wrapped around his fingers there clings
The wet clay of newly birthed forms.

Bowed over the thicket of forms
With a dripping of colour from the sun
He draws the plans of faces
Places the breathing eyes on them
Then searches,
Of these faces, which face is mine?

अमृता . . . इमरोज़

अमृता और इमरोज़ . . . पँजाबी शायरी एका सिक्का उछालो तो head अमृता प्रीतम का चेहरा मिलता है और tail, इमरोज़ की पेन्टिंग।

अमृताजी मुझसे बड़ी थीं और इमरोज़ हम उम्र था। दोनों को उसी ज़माने से जानता हूँ।

ये सोच कर भला लगता है कि अमृताजी ने बहुत बार मुझे नज़्में सुनाने के लिये कहा है . . . वो नसर लिखती थीं। लेकिन ख़ुद सरापा ग़ज़ल थीं।

अमृता . . . इमरोज़

तेरी नज़्म से गुज़रते वक़्त, ख़दशा रहता है
पांव रख रहा हूँ जैसे
गीले लेंडस्केप पर इमरोज़ के!

तेरी नज़्म की इमेज उभरती है
बर्श से रंग टपकने लगते हैं
वो अपने कोरे कैनवास पे नज़्में लिखता है
तुम अपने काग़ज़ों पे नज़्में पेंट करती हो!

Amrita . . . Imroze

Amrita . . . Imroze. Flip the coin of Punjabi poetry in the air and if it falls heads up, you see Amrita's face, and then if it's tails, it's Imroze and his paintings.

Amrita ji was older than me, and Imroze was of my age. I have known both of them since their time together. Thinking of the numerous times that Amrita asked me to recite my poems gives me joy . . . she wrote in prose. But in herself, she was the perfect embodiment of poetry.

Amrita . . . Imroze

When I pass by your poem, I feel afraid
Am I stepping into a wet landscape . . . by Imroze?
Images spring out from your poem
Colours drip off your brush.

He, on his blank canvas, writes a *nazm*
You, on your pages, paint a poem.

वॉन गोग (Van Gogh)

मैं Van Gogh का फ़ैन हुआ, उनकी biography पढ़ कर। इर्विंग स्टोन (Irving Stone) के लिखी। Lust for Life वो किताब इतनी inspiring थी कि जितनी बार जो भी नया एडीशन देखा, ख़रीद लिया। और अक्सर दो दो कापियाँ ख़रीद कर दोस्तों को दीं। और जब पहला मौक़ा हिंदुस्तान से बाहर जाने का लगा तो . . . फ़्राँस गया, उनकी original पेन्टिंग्ज़ देखने के लिये।

Struggling के दिनों में जब भी low महसूस किया, तो वही किताब पढ़ के हौसला बढ़ जाता था। उस किताब की पहली कापी, ख़स्ता सही, पर अब भी मेरे शेल्फ़ पर मौजूद है।

मुझे वॉन गोग पेन्टर की शख़सियत, अक्सर उनकी पेंटिंग (painting) से भी बड़ी लगती है!

वॉन गोग का एक ख़त

तारपिन तेल में कुछ घोली हुई धूप की डलियाँ
मैंने कैनवास पे बिखेरी थी . . . मगर
क्या करूँ, लोगों को उस धूप में रंग दिखते नहीं

मुझसे कहता था 'थियो' चर्च की सर्विस कर लूँ
और उस गिरजे की ख़िदमत में गुज़ारूँ मैं शब-व-रोज़ जहाँ
रात को साया समझते हैं सभी, दिन को सराबों का सफ़र
माद्दे की जो भी हक़ीक़त है नज़र आती नहीं है उनको
मेरी तस्वीरों को कहते हैं . . . तख़ैयुली हैं

ये सब वहमा हैं!

Van Gogh

I became a fan of Van Gogh after reading his biography written by Irving Stone. *Lust for Life*. The book was so inspiring that every time I chanced upon a new edition, I would buy it. Often, I would buy two copies and gift them to my friends. And when the first opportunity to travel outside India came my way, I took myself to France, to view his paintings in the original.

Whenever, during my days of struggle, I felt low, reading the book would boost my morale. Though, undoubtedly, it is somewhat dilapidated, the original copy still stands on my bookshelf. I believe Van Gogh's personality is even greater than his paintings.

Van Gogh's Letter

Some lumps of sunlight, mixed in turpentine
I scattered across my canvas . . . but
What can I do, they can't see the colours
That are lit by that sun.

Pass your days and nights in the service of the Church,
Theo advises,
Where they see the day as a passing shadow and the night as a mirage
Where matter is seen as insubstantial
And my paintings as a whiff of imagination.

मेरे कैनवस पे बने पेड़ की तफ़्सील तो देखें
मेरी तख़्लीक़ ख़ुदावंद के उस पेड़ से कुछ कम तो नहीं है

उसने तो बीज को इक हुक़्म दिया था शायद
पेड़ इस बीज की ही कोख में था, और नुमायाँ भी हुआ
जब कोई टहनी झुकी, पत्ता गिरा, रंग अगर ज़र्द हुआ
तो मुसव्विर ने कहाँ दख़ल दिया
जो हुआ सो हुआ___
मैंने हर शाख़ पे, हर पत्ते की तशकील पे मेहनत की है
उस हक़ीक़त को बयाँ करने में जो हुसने-हक़ीक़त है,
हक़ीक़त के सिवा कुछ भी नहीं

इन दरख़्तों का ये संभला हुआ क़द तो देखो
कैसे ख़ुद्दार हैं ये पेड़ मगर कोई भी मग़रूर नहीं
उनको शेरों की तरह मैंने किया है मौज़ूँ
देखो, तांबे की तरह कैसे दहकते हैं ख़िज़ाँ के पत्ते

'कोयेला कानों' में झोंके हुए मज़दूरों की शकलें
लालटेनें हैं जो शब देर तलक जलती रहीं
आलूओं पर जो गुज़र करते हैं कुछ लोग 'पोटेटो ईटर्ज़'
एक बत्ती के तले एक ही हाले में बँधे लगते हैं सारे

मैंने देखा था, हवा खेतों से जब भाग रही थी
अपने कैनवस पे उसे रोक लिया
'रोलां' वो 'चिट्ठी रसाँ' और वो स्कूल में पढ़ता लड़का,
'ज़र्द ख़ातून', पड़ोसन थी मेरी
फ़ानी लोगों की तग़ैयुर से बचा कर, उन्हें कैनवस पे तवारीख़
की उम्रें दी हैं!

सालहा-साल ये तस्वीरें बनायीं मैंने

This is all a misconception
Let them but see the details of the tree on my canvas
My creation is no less than God's

Perhaps He had only ordered a seed to grow
And the tree nestled in the womb of the seed appeared
If a branch dipped or a leaf fell or grew pale
The Creator paid no heed
It was just as it was.

I have laboured on every branch and every leaf shape
To reveal the beauty of the real.

Look at the stance my trees take
They stand so proud, but without arrogance
I have balanced them like the lines of a poem
Look how the autumn leaves glow like copper.

The faces of the labourers in the 'coal mines'
Burn like lanterns deep into the night
Some, who sustain themselves on potatoes, the 'Potato Eaters'
Seem to be encircled in the lamplight's halo

When I saw the wind rushing through the fields
I trapped it on my canvas.

'Roulin' the 'postman' and the young schoolboy
The 'Zard Khatoon', that noble lady, my neighbour
Saving them from being altered by death
I have given them eternal life on my canvas.

मेरे नक़्क़ाद मगर बोले नहीं
उनकी ख़ामोशी खटकती थी मेरे कानों में

उसपे तस्वीर बनाते हुए इक कव्वे की वो चीख़ पुकार
कव्वा खिड़की पे नहीं, सीधा मेरे कान पे आ बैठता था,
कान ही काट दिया है मैंने!

मेरे पैलेट पे रखी धूप तो अब सूख गयी है
'तारपिन' तेल में इक घोला था सूरज मैंने
आसमाँ उसका बिछाने के लिये लेकिन उस वक़्त
चँद बालिश्त का कैनवस भी मेरे पास नहीं!

मैं यहाँ 'रेमी' में हूँ
'सेंट रेमी' के दवाख़ाने में थोड़ी सी मरम्मत
के लिये भरती हुआ हूँ
उनका कहना है कई पुरज़े मेरे ज़हन के
अब ठीक नहीं
मुझे लगता है वो पहले से सवा तेज़ हैं अब!

Year after year I continued to create paintings
But my critics said nothing
Their silence rattled against my ears.

And then, while I was working on my canvas
The shrill sound of a crow cawing loud . . .

Not on the windowsill, but on my ear
The bird would perch,
I cut the ear off!

I am here at Remy now
Admitted into St Remy's Hospital
For some repair work
Their diagnosis is that
Many parts of my brain are damaged
Though I believe it is sharper now than it was ever before.

अशोक भौमिक

ज़रा सोचो अशोक भौमिक . . .
ख़ुदायी तुमको देते और कहते,
ज़रा अपनी तरह से पेंट कर के तो दिखाओ ज़िंदगी को
तो ब्लैक एँड व्हाईट (black & white) से तुम रँग भरते,
सियाही से लिखे होते सभी लम्हों के चेहरे
झपकती पलकों में दिन रात कितने साफ़ दिखते
बड़ा आसान होता आँखें सूरज से मिलाना !

ज़मीं पर गोल, चौरस कैनवास पहने हुजूम आते
इरादे, मसले कुछ ज़िंदगी के
तिकोनी शक्ल लेकर,
उलझते, भीड़ में भिड़ते हुए कुछ लोग होते
तुम अपने आप ही में इक ज़माना होते उसमें !

कहीं फुटपाथ पर, इक बादशाह अर्चिन (urchin) बिठा रखा है तुमने
उड़ाता है पतँगें रात दिन की
नहीं है फ़र्क़ दोनों की सियाही में !

तुम्हारे कोल माइनर्ज़ (coal miners),
न जाने कौन सी कोयेलों की खानों से
निकाले हैं वो तुमने

वो पत्थराये हुए चेहरे,
किसी चूल्हे में झोंके जायेंगे तो लाल होंगे !

Ashok Bhawmik

Just imagine, Ashok Bhawmik,
If creation were presented to you, saying
Show us life painted the way you would colour it
You would fill it with black and white
Portray all the moments in ink
How clearly the fluttering eyelids would reflect night and day
It would be so easy to exchange glances with the sun.

Wearing round and square canvases, crowds would throng the ground
Intentions, problems sporting triangular faces,
Would brush shoulders caught in the crowd
You would be an era unto yourself, in it.

Somewhere, on the footpath, you have placed a 'king urchin'
He flies the kites of night and day
There is no difference in the ink of both.

Your 'Coal Miners'
Who knows which mines you have pulled them from
Their stone-etched faces
If thrown into an oven
Would turn red.

नुकीली, तीखी आँखों में,
कमानें दर्द की खींचे हुए चलते हैं जब,
अशोक भौमिक . . .
तुम्हारी पेन्टिंग़्ज़ (paintings) में मुझको हिंदुस्तान दिखता है!

Those elongated, sharp eyes,
Carry well-strung bows of pain
Ashok Bhawmik . . .
I see India contained in your paintings.

कलबुर्गी

कोई रिश्ता नहीं था। न देखा, न मिला।
बस क़लम के सगे थे हम!

कलबुर्गी . . .

मरा नहीं वो . . .
वो और था कोई जो मरा है
वहीं पे दहलीज़ पर पड़ा है

किसी ने घँटी बजायी घर की
वो अपने बच्चों को
क, ख, ज, झ, सिखा रहा था
उठा, गया, कुँडी खोली घर की . . .
और एक आवाज़ गूँजी, गोली की, आसमाँ में
'विचार' था उसके सर में कोई
जो बोलता था . . .
'विचार' दहलीज़ पर पड़ा है!

Kalburgi

There was never any relationship. We had never seen each other, nor met. Only related through our writings.

Kalburgi . . .

He did not die,
That was someone else who died
He's lying there, across the threshold.

Someone rang the bell at his house
He was teaching his children the alphabet
He rose, and went, opened the latch of his door
And the sound of a bullet echoed in the skies.

He held an idea in his mind
Which would resound loud
That idea is lying there, across the threshold . . .

सुवर्णा

ये लड़की हमेशा रात के वक़्त आसमाँ पे मिली। कभी ज़मीन पर चलते नहीं देखा। वो एयर-
होस्टेस थी। बम्बई से भोपाल . . . कभी भोपाल से बम्बई . . . बस ये दो शहर पिरोती रहती थी।
एक ही एयरलाइन चलती थी तब 'इन्डियन एयरलाइन'!

किसी तार पे बहती बूँद की तरह आती जाती थी। पता नहीं कब टपक गयी। ज़मीन पर!
कहीं जज़्ब हो गयी! बस गयी! 'इन्डियन एयरलाइन' के पते पर ये नज़्म उसे भेजी थी। पता नहीं
मिली भी के नहीं। यूँ भी कुछ लोग मिले, जो बड़े सगे लगे।

सुवर्णा

फ़लक में देखे थे उड़ते उड़ते
वो शहर शब के
वो सांवली रौशनी के पीछे से जगमगाते
जज़ीरे शब के
वो दो जज़ीरे
वो 'बनलता सेन सी सुवर्णा' की काली काली बड़ी सी आँखें

Suvarna

I have always met this girl in the sky. Never seen her walking on the ground. She was an air hostess. Bombay to Bhopal or Bhopal to Bombay . . . she would thread her way through these two cities. At that time, there was only one airline . . . Indian Airlines. Like a drop of water on a wire, she would travel to and fro.

I don't know when she dropped to the earth. Got absorbed. Settled down.

I had sent this poem to her address at Indian Airlines. Wonder if she even got it.

Even thus, I meet some people, who seem like kinsfolk.

Suvarna

I have seen while flying
The cities of the night
Glittering behind the dusky light
The islands of the night
The two islands, those big black eyes like those of Banalata Sen.

हवा-नवरदी में आते जाते
हमेशा परवाज़ में मिली है
पिरोती रहती है शहर दोनों
कि जैसे आँखें पिरो के रखती हैं इक नज़र में
वो कहकशाँ के सिरों पे उड़ते
परिन्दे शब के
नये नये एक और 'नोवा' से पैदा होते
सितारे शब के
दो रात बहनें
वो 'बनलता सेन सी सुवर्णा' की काली काली बड़ी सी आँखें!

जो सात सैयारों ने बिलो के निथारे लम्हे
छलक के फिर कहकशाँ की गर्दिश में खो ना जायें

हमेशा मिलती हो आसमाँ की उड़ान में तुम
कभी हवाओं के इस दबाव से नीचे उतरो
ज़मीं पे पांव लगा के देखो
ज़मीं पे भी हैं तुम्हारी आँखों से कुछ समंदर
अगरचे इतने सियाह नहीं हैं
न इतने गहरे!

While voyaging up and down in the air
I always met her on the flight.

She kept knitting the two cities
Like she knits the look from both her eyes.

The two birds of the night flying to the rhythm of the Milky Way
Two stars of the night, born from the explosion of a new Nova
Two night sisters like the eyes of Banalata Sen.*

Seven planets churned Time to produce the twin moments
May they not get lost among the stars of the Milky Way

You always meet me in the space of the sky,
Come down from the confines of the air sometime
Touch your feet to the earth and see
On earth also, there are oceans like your eyes
Perhaps not as dark, or as deep.

---

* Banalata Sen is a famous poem by the renowned Bengali poet, Jibanananda Das,
  in which he mentions the dark eyes of Banalata Sen.

ख़ान्दोमान

मैं भूटान में ख़ान्दोमान से मिला। उसका लहजा और गुफ़्तूगू का अँदाज़े आम तौर पर भूटानी था। अगरचा मैंने सुना था कि उसने न्यू योरक (New York) में तालीम हासिल की थी। लेकिन मैं न तो उसके बारे में सोच सकता था और न ही उसका तसव्वुर कर सकता था—स्वाये भूटान के मँज़र नामे के!

ख़ान्दोमान

पहाड़ों में मिली थी वो . . .
जड़ी बूटी के जैसे अपनी मिट्टी से जुड़ी थी
वही पहनावा 'किरा', नाक में नथ की जगह, तिन्का फसाये
जड़ों सी उँगलियाँ पैरों की फैली फैली रहती थीं
उसे जब देखा, नंगे पांव ही देखा
वो जितनी खिड़कियाँ खुलती थीं घर की, सब में दिखती थी
कभी वो घास में बैठी,
न जाने नाख़ुनों से क्या उठाती थी कि जैसे धूप चुनती हो
कभी तालाब में पांव डुबोये
बताशे बुलबुलों के फूटती रहती थी पैरों से

Khandoman

I met Khandoman in Bhutan. Her diction and tone and disposition were typically Bhutanese. Though I had heard she had studied in New York. But I could neither think of her nor imagine her except against the landscape of Bhutan.

Khandoman

I met her in the mountains
As much a part of nature as plants are
Her dress, the traditional 'kira',
A stick of straw fixed in her nose instead of a nose ring
Like roots, her toes would be splayed
Whenever I saw her, she was barefoot
She would be visible from every open window in the house.

Sometimes sitting on the grass
Who knows what she would pick up with her nails,
As if plucking rays of sunlight
At times with her feet dipped in water
She would kick at the globed bubbles, bursting them

बुलाया भी तो यूँ आकर खड़ी रहती थी वो गर्दन झुकाये
हवा का हुक्म सुन कर, शाख़ झुक जाती है जैसे

वहाँ के पौधों पेड़ों ही से वो पैदा हुई थी
पहाड़ों में मिली थी वो . . . मैं जब 'भूटान' में था!

If summoned, she would come and stand, head bowed
Like a bough bending when it hears the wind's decree.

She was born of Nature, like the saplings and trees there
I met her in the mountains . . . when I was in Bhutan.

पोमो—आनी चोईंग ड्रोलमा
(Pomo—Ani Choying Drolma)

नन (nun) कहते ही, जोगन का ख़्याल आता है। Ani नन है, जोगन नहीं!

जोगन सुन कर, त्याग और बैराग का ख़्याल आता है। नन, बहुत कुछ त्याग कर भी, समाज से जुड़ी रहती है। Ani . . . एक musical concert में मिली थी। आँखें बँद कर के सुर लगाती थी तो साध्वी लगती थी। न होंट हिलते थे, न गर्दन! इबारत (दुआ) जैसा ऊँचा सुर कैसे लगा लेती थी? 'तिब्बत' से निकली, नेपाल में बसी ये लड़की तेरहा साल की उम्र में नन हो गयी। शराबी और ज़ालिम बाप के मुक्के सहते सहते, क़सम खा ली थी, किसी मर्द से वास्ता न रखेगी।

तब ग्यारह साल की थी। माँ ने कह दिया, 'भाग जा—नन हो जा!'

ये नन अब नेपाल में मोटर साईकल पर सफ़र करती है और लावारिस बच्चों के लिये स्कूल और हसपताल चलाती है।

नन होने की वार्दात उसकी किताब में पढ़ी। एक बार मिला हूँ—सुना है—पढ़ा है—फिर मिलूँगा—यक़ीनन!

पोमो—आनी चोईंग ड्रोलमा

बहुत बंजर लगी थी रात पहली, मौनेस्ट्री (monastery) में
अकेली भी कभी पहले किसी कमरे की मुट्ठी में न सोयी थी
बड़ी वज़नी लगी उस रात ख़ामोशी

Pomo—Ani Choying Drolma

Say the word 'nun' and an ascetic comes to mind. Ani is a nun, not an ascetic.

The word ascetic makes you think of sacrifice and detachment. But a nun, despite sacrificing a lot, remains connected with society. I met Ani at a musical concert. When she closed her eyes to sing a note, she looked like a *sadhvi*. Her lips did not move, nor did her throat. Yet, how could she sing notes that soared like a prayer? The Tibetan girl who had settled in Nepal became a nun at thirteen! After suffering her alcoholic and abusive father's blows repeatedly, she swore never to have any relationships with men.

She was eleven then. Her mother had said, 'Run away. Become a nun.'

This nun now rides about Nepal on a motorcycle and runs a school and hospital for orphan children.

I read about the incident that made her into a nun in her book. I have met her once—heard her—read her. I will meet her again, surely!

Pomo—Ani Choying Drolma

How desolate the night seemed in the monastery
I had never slept alone in the fist of a room
The silence seemed heavy that night

अकेली थी मैं कमरे में
चिपक के ठँडी सी दीवार से मैं रीढ़ की . . .
हड्डी को महसूस कर रही थी
कि इससे पहले मुक्कों से बजा करती थी ये हड्डी!

मेरा सर मुँडने से पहले रेज़र से
किसी 'शैम्पू' से मेरे बाल धोये और काटे थे

फ़क़त एहसास देने के लिये शायद
तुम्हारी कैंचली धोकर उतारी जा रही है

गुरूब होते हुए सूरज को मैंने
मेरे तेरहा साल ले जाते हुए देखा
उतारे कपड़े जो दो तीन टुकड़ों में पहन रखे थे मैंने
लिफ़ाफ़े की तरह पहना अनाबी रंग का चोला!

टपकते छत से कोई बूँद टपकी,
मेरे सर पे और गूंजी
न विवाहिता थी, न विधवा थी
कंवारी भी नहीं थी मैं
तो क्या थी?

ख़ला के एक टुकड़े से जुड़ी
ख़ला का बुलबुला थी मैं
मुझे एहसास था 'नन' (nun) हो गयी हूँ मैं!

ख़ला में तैरता इक बुलबुला हो तुम 'पोमो'
किरन सूरज की तुमको छू रही है और चमकती है!

I was alone in the room
And sticking to the cold wall
I was aware of my spine
Which before now had resounded in response to blows.

Before shaving my head with a razor,
My hair had been shampooed and cut
Perhaps just to make me realize
Your mortal coils are being washed and shed.

I watched the setting sun take
The thirteen years of my life away.
Taking off the two or three shreds of clothes
I had been wearing
I donned the envelope of the maroon robe.

A drop from the leaking roof touched my head
And resounded
Neither was I wife, nor widow
Nor was I a maiden
Then, what was I?

Linked to the vast void
I was just a bubble in it
I understood I had now
Become a nun.

'You are a bubble swimming in the void, Pomo
The ray of the sun is resting on you, and shining.'

महात्मा गांधी

बापू थे 'बापू' !

मैंने क़रीब से देखा है उन्हें !

हर शाम प्राथना के बाद, बिरला हाऊस से नशर होने वाला, (मतलब ब्रोड कास्ट होने वाला . . .) भाषण भी सुना है। अपने अब्बू के साथ बैठ कर !

बापू

सवा गज़ आसमाँ ओढ़े हुए सर पे
बदन पर एक लँगोटी लपेटे
वो पूजा के लिये निकला था बाहर
किसी ने आगे बढ़ कर
तमंचा रख दिया सीने पे ये कह के
तुम्हारी राय से सहमत नहीं हैं हम !

तमंचा चल रहा है
वो राय मरती नहीं है !

Mahatma Gandhi

Bapu was 'Bapu'. I've seen him up close. And his daily evening broadcasts from Birla House that followed after his prayers, I listened to them too. With my father.

Bapu

One-quarter yard of sky wrapped around his head
With only a loin cloth wrapped around his form
He had stepped out for prayers
Someone, moving forward
Stuck a pistol in his chest, saying
We don't agree with your idea.

The shots continue
The idea doesn't die.

राजीव गांधी

बम्बई में, 'अँधेरी' के इलाक़े में, एक इन्दु भाई की म्युज़िक सिस्टम (music system) बनाने वाली फ़ेक्ट्री में, एक पायलट से मिला था। बड़ी ख़ूबसूरत, छोटी सी गुफ़्तगू हुई थी। मेरी ख़रीद में उन्होंने सलह भी दी थी, जो मैंने मान ली। मैंने पहचाना नहीं।

जाते हुए मुसाफ़ा भी किया। मुसाफ़ा मतलब shake hands। जाने के बाद इन्दु भाई ने बताया, वो राजीव गांधी थे। और फिर तब मिला जब वो हिंदुस्तान के वज़ीरे आज़म थे। यानी प्राइम मिनिस्ट्र।

एक ख़ुबरू, मासूम, हैन्डसम, मुकम्मिल हिंदुस्तानी। बहुत बुरा हुआ, जो हुआ।

राजीव गांधी

साया एक धूप का था
और उस धूप के टुकड़े को बड़ी तेज़ी से
कोहसारों पर चढ़ते हुए देखा था सभी ने
राह पेचीदा थी उस धूप के टुकड़े के लिये
आढ़ी तिरछी सी चट्टानें थीं, कहीं काई की फिसलन
और कुछ खोखले से पेड़ भी थे, जिनकी जड़ों में
वक़्त के टूटे हिए दाँत पड़े थे
उनकी परछाइयाँ रस्ते में पड़ी हाँप रही थीं

Rajiv Gandhi

In Indu Bhai's factory that made 'Cosmic' music systems in Andheri, Bombay, I met a pilot. We had a short but sweet conversation. He even advised me on what I should purchase. But I did not recognize him.

As he was leaving he shook hands with me. After he had left, Indu Bhai told me that he was Rajiv Gandhi. I met him again, when he had become India's prime minister.

An innocent, handsome, perfect Hindustani.

Whatever happened was a terrible thing.

Rajiv Gandhi

The sun's shadow he was
And everyone had watched that piece of sun climbing swiftly over the
    mountains
The route was complicated, for the piece of sun . . .
Jagged, crooked peaks and slippery routes of old moss
And some hollow trees, with Time's broken teeth
Lying hidden among the roots
Their shadows lay across his path, panting.

सब ने रोका था मगर धूप का टुकड़ा था, जवाँ साल अभी
गर्दनें खींच के कँधों से उठाली थीं सभी ने
सब उसे देख रहे थे
सब को उम्मीद थी, कोहसार की चोटी पे पहुँच कर
वो बहा लायेगा, इक्सिवी सदी का दरया

इक धमाका सा हुआ
और इक लम्हा फटा
और झुलसा हुआ वो धूप का टुकड़ा
आग के टुकड़ों में बहता हुआ वादी में गिरा!

Everyone had stopped him, but a sun's ray he was, yet young
Stretching their necks from their shoulders
All were watching him
All were hopeful, that scaling the mountain's peak he would
Bring down the twenty-first century like a river.

An explosion occurred
A moment was torn asunder
And the scorched piece of the sun
Flowed down to the earth with shards of burning fire.

नील आर्मस्ट्राँग (Neil Armstrong)

पूरी नसले आदम का नुमाईन्दा चाँद पर गया था। (Representation of the human race.)
पहली बार। जब हमेशा के लिये ज़मीं छोड़ गया तो हम में से किसी ने याद न किया उसे। हिंदुस्तान
के किसी अदीब, या शायर ने कुछ न लिक्खा। क्या हमारा कुछ न लगता था?

नील आर्मस्ट्राँग (Neil Armstrong)

कितनी बार अकेले छत पे जाके चाँद को देखता था
और मज़ाक़ किया करता था . . .
'बायाँ पैर ज़मीं पर है और दायाँ पैर वहीं रखा है यार,
हाथ बढ़ाओ . . .
झुक के हाथ पकड़ लो यार और ऊपर खींच लो
एक पैर पे खड़े खड़े मैं थकने लगा हूँ!'

पहला पाँव जिसने चाँद पे रखा था
दूसरा पाँव आज ज़मीं से उठा लिया, और
चाँद से आगे निकल गया है!

* Neil Armstrong died on 25 August 2012

Neil Armstrong

Representing the entire human race, he stepped on the moon.
For the very first time. When he left the earth for good, none
of us spared him a thought. No Indian poet or scholar wrote a
eulogy for him. Did he mean nothing to us?

Neil Armstrong

Innumerable times he would go up to the terrace to look at the moon
And say jokingly,
'The left foot is on the earth and the right one is right there, my friend
Stretch your hand
And bending down, hold my hand, and pull me up
It's tiring to keep standing on one foot.'

He who placed the first foot on the moon
Has lifted his other foot off the earth
And gone far beyond the moon.

अँड्रू फ्यूस्टेल (Andrew Feustel)

जन्नत अगर 'ऊपर' है कहीं, तो अँड्रू फ्यूस्टेल उसके पास हो कर आया है। छ महीने रह कर आया है। वो भी जीते जी!

अँड्रू फ्यूस्टेल (Andrew Feustel)

स्पेस स्टेशन पर टांगा हुआ मैं तैर रहा था
मैं अँड्रू फ्यूस्टेल (Andrew Feustel)
मध्दम मध्दम रौशन एक ख़ला अँदर
देख रहा था
कायेनात में झूलते सैयारों की पेंगें
झुमर भरे सितारों के
कहकशाँ की पगडँडी से निकल रहे थे
भँवर कई चौराहों के!

जानता था जन्नत की राह नज़दीक है लेकिन
लौट आया मैं
अभी ज़मीं पर काम बहुत थे!

* Endeavour Shuttle in Space.
† Andrew Feustel—ख़ला में स्पेस पर मरम्मत के लिये गया था और छ माह तक वहाँ रहा।

Andrew Feustel

If heaven is up there somewhere, then Andrew Feustel has been close to it. Six months has he spent there and returned. That too while still alive.

Andrew Feustel

Hanging by the space station, I was swimming
I, Andrew Feustel
Inside a softly lit vacant space
I was seeing
The universe and its swinging planets
Chandeliers of stars passing through the pathway of the Milky Way
To form whirlpools, streaking out in different directions.

I knew the path to heaven was close, but . . .
I returned.
There was much left to be done on earth.

---

* Endeavour Shuttle in Space.
† Andrew Feustel went into space for undertaking repair work and stayed there for six months.

IV

अब्बू

ये मेरे अब्बू हैं! मेरे पिताजी! मैं उन्हें अब्बू कह के बुलाता नहीं था। लेकिन इस नाम से याद करना बहुत प्यारा लगता है . . . हमेशा!

अब्बू

अब्बू . . .
बहुत कुछ है जो कहना रह गया है आपसे,
होते तो कहता . . .
बहुत मायूस थे मुझसे, कि मेरी शायरी
ले डूबेगी मुझको
अभी तक तैर रहा हूँ मैं अब्बू!
मगर साहिल पे आने की तमन्ना भी नहीं अब
मुझे मालूम है कि आप साहिल छोड़ कर अब जा चुके हैं!

Abbu

This is my Abbu . . . my father. I never used to call him Abbu.
But I love to call him by this name in my memories of him . . .
always.

Abbu

Abbu!
There's so much that was left unsaid,
I would tell you, if you were here.

You were very downcast thinking,
My poetry would be my undoing, sink me
I am still swimming, Abbu
With no desire now to reach the shore.
Now that I know that you have
Abandoned the shore and gone away.

अब्बू

उतनी ही उम्र को आ पहुँचा हूँ अब्बू
जितनी उम्र पे आख़िर आख़िर, तुम मुझको कहते थे . . .
'ये आवारगी छोड़ो, कोई 'चज' का काम करो!'

अख़बार में लेकिन नाम मेरा पढ़ लेते थे तो
आँखें चमक उठती थीं
सारा दिन अख़बार तुम्हारे हाथ में रहता था
उतनी ही उम्र को आ पहुँचा हूँ अब्बू
ख़ुद से अक्सर कह लेता हूँ
'ये आवारगी छोड़ो, कोई ढंग का काम करो!'
लेकिन अब्बूजी . . .
अपनी किताब में, आपका ज़िक्र पढ़ता हूँ तो,
मेरी आँखें चमक उठती हैं!

Abbu

I have reached the exact same age now,
At which age, towards the end, you would say to me,
'Leave this aimlessness, find something worthwhile to do.'

Yet, when you read my name in the newspapers,
Your eyes would light up
You'd carry the paper in your hands through the day.

I've reached just the same age, Abbu
Often I tell myself,
Let go of this aimlessness, do something worthwhile.
Yet, Abbuji,
When in my book, I find you mentioned
My eyes light up.

माँ

'माँ' लफ़्ज़ में बड़ी ममता है। माँ से भी ज़्यादा। बोलते ही नाभी में कुछ पिघलने लगता है।
नज़्मों गीतों में भी हम फ़ौरन लिख देते हैं।
'ले के गोदी में लोरी सुनाती थी माँ चाहे ना भी सुनी हो!'
कूड़े के ढ़ेर पर फेंक गये बच्चे भी किसी एक चेहरे को तलाश तो करते होंगे!
अच्छा है! आईने के सामने खड़े हो जाओ, और चेहरे में ढूँढो उसे!

माँ

तुझ को पहचानूँ भी कैसे, तुझे देखा ही नहीं
ढूँडा करता हूँ तुझे अपने ही चेहरे में कहीं

लोग कहते हैं मेरी आँखें, मेरी माँ सी हैं
यूँ तो लबरेज़ हैं पानी से मगर प्यासी हैं

कान में छेद है, पैदाइशी आया होगा
तूने मन्नत के लिये, कान छेदाया होगा

Ma

There's so much mamta in the word Ma. More than in a mother herself. Just saying the word starts off a churning in the navel.

Easily we imagine and write in songs and poems, 'Holding the child in her lap, the mother would sing a lullaby.' Though we may never have heard them.

Even the children thrown into the rubbish heap must often search for that one face.

It is good. Stand in front of the mirror, and in that face, search for hers.

Ma

How will I recognize you; whom I have never seen
In my own face I look for you with eyes keen

They say my eyes are like my mother's
Though brimming with liquid, their thirst can be seen

My ears are pierced, perhaps from birth
You must have had yours pierced after pledging a troth

सामने दाँतों में वक़्फ़ा है, तेरे भी होगा
एक चक्कर तेरे पांव के तले भी होगा

जाने किस जलदी में थी जन्म दिया, दौड़ गई
क्या ख़ुदा देख लिया था जो मुझे छोड़ गई

मिल कर देखता हूँ मिल जाये कोई मुझ सी कहीं
तेरे बिन उपरी लगती है कभी सारी ज़मीं

तुझ को पहचानूँ भी कैसे, तुझे देखा ही नहीं
ढूँडा करता हूँ तुझे अपने ही चेहरे में कहीं

The gap in my front teeth, must have been in yours too
And the same circle must have shown on your sole too

Wonder what your hurry was, you gave birth and chose to flee
Did you see God himself, that you had to leave me?

How will I recognize you; whom I have never seen
In my own face I look for you with eyes keen.

सेल्फ़ पोटरेट (Self-Portrait)

मुझे तो आप जानते ही हैं!

सेल्फ़ पोटरेट (Self-Portrait)

रोज़ ही आइने पर लिख कर जाता हूँ मैं
सारे चिन्ह और चेहरा अपना
लौटूं तो पहचन्ने में कोई भूल न हो . . .
लेकिन रोज़ बदल जाता है कुछ न कुछ
एक मोम्मा बना हुआ हूँ अपने लिये
देखूं तो . . .
पहले से हिर्स कुछ और ज़्यादा है आँखों में
उमीद की धड़कन बढ़ी हुई है
और चिन्ता के चिन्ह ज़्यादा गहरे होने लगे हैं

पक्का रँग है, काला तो, सुनते हैं
फिर भी . . .
जाने क्यों बालों का रँग उतरने लगा है

एक मोम्मा बना हुआ है, आईने में!

Self-Portrait

I'm sure you know me. In case you don't, read my poems, and
you will make my acquaintance.

Self-Portrait

On the mirror, every day, I record
My face and all its discerning features
So that I make no mistake in knowing it
When I return.
Yet, something or the other changes
On each succeeding day.

A puzzle of sorts has emerged

I observe . . .
A shade more of lust in the eyes
Than was there before
Reflecting heightened expectations
And worry running deeper through more lines.

I've heard that black is a permanent colour,
And yet,
I wonder why it's fading off my hair
A puzzle indeed, has been etched on my mirror.

शोनू

हमने देखी है उन आँखों की महकती ख़ुशबू
हाथ से छू के इसे रिश्तों का इलज़ाम न दो
सिर्फ़ एहसास है ये, रूह से महसूस करो!

शोनू

अजब रेशम का रिश्ता है
अजब रेशम की सुतली है
फिसल जाती है खींचो तो
लिपट जाती है जब छोड़ो
गिरह ऐसी लगी है जैसे कि 'नाभी' का रिश्ता हो
जो कट जाने पे भी फिर उम्र भर कटते नहीं है!

Shonu

I have seen the wafting fragrance of those eyes
Touch it not with your hand, do not heap the burden of a
relationship on it
It's just a feeling; experience it with your soul

Shonu

Such a strange silken bond
Such a strange silken thread
Slips if you tug at it
Binds you if you let go of it
Knotted like the knot of the umbilical cord
Which though severed, remains linked through a lifetime.

बोस्की

मेरी बच्ची का एक और नाम भी है 'बोस्की'!

बोस्की

व़क़्त को आते न जाते न गुज़रते देखा
न उतरते हुए देखा कभी अल्हाम की सूरत
जमा होते हुए इक जगह मगर देखा है

शायद आया था वो ख़्वाबों से दबे पांव ही
और जब आया ख़्यालों को भी एहसास ना था
आँख का रंग तुलू होते हुए देखा जिस दिन
मैंने चूमा था मगर वक़्त को पहचाना ना था

चंद तुतलाये हुए बोलों में आहट भी सुनी
दूध का दाँत गिरा था तो वहाँ भी देखा
बोस्की बेटी मेरी, चिकनी सी रेशम की डली
लिपटी लिपटाई हुई रेशमी तागों में पड़ी थी
मुझको एहसास नहीं था के वहाँ वक़्त पड़ा है

Bosky

My child has one more name, Bosky.

Bosky

Time. Not seen it coming, going or passing by
Nor seen the face of dreams on earth
But I have seen Time
Gathering in a contained space.

Perhaps it came soft-footed out of my dreams
Not letting even my thoughts be aware of its coming
The day I watched the sunrise in her eyes
I kissed Time but failed to recognize it.

I heard its footsteps in the lisping words
Saw it too where the milk teeth fell
Bosky, my daughter, delicate as a silk petal
Lay wrapped in layers in her silken hammock
I did not fathom that it was Time lying there.

पालना खोल के जब मैंने उतारा था उसे बिस्तर पर
लोरी के बोलों से इक बार छुआ था उसको
बढ़ते नाख़ुनों में हर बार ताशा भी था
चूड़ियाँ चढ़ती उतरती थीं कलाई पर मुसलसल
और हाथों से उतरती कभी चढ़ती थीं किताबें
मुझको मालूम नहीं था कि वहाँ वक़्त लिखा है

वक़्त को आते न जाते न गुज़रते देखा
जमा होते हुए देखा मगर उसको मैंने
इस बरस बोस्की अठारह बरस की होगी!

Lifting her from the cradle, when I placed her on the bed
I touched her gently with a lullaby's soft words
Trimmed each time her growing nails
Bangles would unceasingly travel up and down wrists
And books would climb into her hands and then slip down . . .
I did not realize Time was written in them.

I have not seen Time coming, going or passing by
But I have seen it gathered in a place
This year Bosky turns eighteen.

बोस्की और गोविंद

मेरी बच्ची है 'बुच्चू'—और गोविंद मेरे दामाद हैं! बेटे ही हुए नां!

बोस्की और गोविंद

9 जनवरी 2000 की बात है!

सात उफ़क़ खोल के महंदी लगे पाँव लेकर
मैंने देखा है तुझे जाते हुए घर से निकल कर
चढ़ते सूरज की तरफ़ गोविंद का हाथ पकड़ कर!

वक़्त तो वक़्त है जानां बुच्चू
मैंने जितना भी संभाला था, कल्सी में तुझे भर के दिया है
इक सदी और तुम्हें भरनी होगी
इक सदी तुम्हें जीना है, जीना होगा
और तुम दोनों को, हर रोज़ उफ़क़ खोलना होगा
रोज़ सूरज तुम्हें एक और उगाना होगा!

Bosky And Govind

My daughter is 'Buchkoo'
And Govind, my son-in-law!
Isn't he a son after all?

Bosky and Govind

Remembering 9 January 2000

Crossing seven horizons on mehndi-red feet
You went out of the house, I watched as
Holding Govind's hand you stepped towards
The rising sun.

Time is just time, darling Buchkoo
I filled whatever I had gathered in a *kalsi*
And gave it to you.
You have to fill it now for a century more
You have a century more to live, you must
Each day, you both, pushing open the horizon
Each day, grow a new sun.

बोस्की और गोविंद

तितलियाँ पौधों पे उड़ती हैं
सर्गम की तरह, 'आरोही' और 'अवरोहीं' सी
मेघ ठाठ का राग लगा है
बादल लँबी तान के पलटे लेता है तो
झूम उठते हैं दूर दूर तक पाम के पेड़
बोस्की और गोविंद के साथ
औरंगाबाद में
जशन है अब के जन्म दिन का!

Bosky and Govind

Butterflies dance over the flowers
Like the notes of music they hover
Rising and swooping like 'arohi' and 'avrohi'
Of a raag in Megh *thaat*.
When the cloud sings its long drawn *paltas*
Even the far-off palm trees toss about in ecstasy.
With Bosky and Govind, in Aurangabad
This year's birthday is being celebrated!

मेघना

बोस्की बड़ी हो गयी। अब 'मेघना' है।

मेघना

समंदर, देख रहा था,
समंदर से, मेरी अमृत की कुँभी आने वाली थी
समंदर कर्वटें लेता था, रह रह कर, तो बल पड़ते थे पानी में
मेरी बच्ची की नाज़ुक कोख से टीसें गुज़रती थीं
मुझे उस वक़्त डर लगता था 'अमृत' माँगने से

उसे जब कपकपी आती थी तो मैं काँप जाता था
वो प्यासी थी
मगर पानी मना था, बर्फ़ की डलियाँ फिरायी जा रही थीं
ख़ुशक होंटों पर

समंदर अपने पानी में ही ग़ौते खाने लगता था
समंदर काट के 'कुँभी' निकालो
न काटोगे तो मर जायेगी बच्ची!

Meghna

Bosky has grown up. She is Meghna, now.

Meghna

I was watching the sea
My pot of nectar was to emerge from the sea
Sporadically the sea would toss and turn
Making the water convulse in pain.
As spasms racked my daughter's delicate womb
I was afraid of asking for the nectar.

Every shiver that went through her body
Would make me tremble
She was thirsty . . .
But water was forbidden, ice cubes were touched
to parched lips.

The sea was tossing in its agony
Tear open the sea and draw out the *kumbhi*
Cut it open or my child will die!

मेरे 'अमृत की कुँभी' को वो जब गोदी में लेकर अब खिलाती है
मेरे अँदर से कोई मर्द कहता है:
'तुम्हें तौफ़ीक़ ही न थी,
कि तुम ये दर्द सहते, और इक इंसान की तख़्लीक़ करते!'

(समय के जन्म पर)

When she holds my 'pot of nectar' on her lap and feeds it now
A voice emerges from the male in my heart
'You never were capable enough
To bear this pain, and create life.'

(On Samay's birth)

समय

मेरा नवासा है। मेरी इकलोती बेटी का इकलोता बेटा।

समय

समय !
रोये नहीं जब पैदा हुए तुम
कु कु करते मिले थे तुम
जुगनू की तरह हल्की हल्की, चमकीं थीं महीन आवाज़ की बूँदें
रेढ़ी जैसी 'ट्रोली' पर रख कर लाये थे हमें मिलाने, आपके पापा . . .

थोड़ी देर में 'माँ' आयीं तो फिर उसकी आँखों में देखा
तुम ही तुम थे, छलक रहे थे
वो कांप रही थी
उसका कांपना मुझसे क्यों देखा न गया?
कांप रही थी जैसे उसको ख़ाली कर के भेज दिया हो !

Samay

He is my grandson. My only daughter's only son.

Samay

Samay . . .
You did not cry when you were born
Made 'kukun kukun' sounds when we met
Glittering sounds from your thin voice
Shining like ethereal glow worms
On a trolley with castors, your papa had brought you
To meet me.

When 'ma' came after a while,
I could see only you and you alone
In her eyes, sparkling, spilling out
She was a-trembling
Why was I unable to bear her trembling?
She was trembling as if she had been emptied and sent back.

समय

छोटा सा 'प्लेनेट' समझा था, पैदा हुआ है
मेरे सोलर सिस्टम में!
मेरा नवासा!
डेढ़ साल का है और ये महसूस होता है
आफ़ताब वो है और हम सब . . .
उसके 'प्लेनेट' हैं, उसके गिर्द घूमा करते हैं
मोह में 'ग्रेविटी' जैसी ताकत होती है!

Samay

A tiny planet I realized, has been born
In my 'solar system'
My daughter's son.
He's a year-and-a-half, and we realize
He is the sun and all of us
his planets, orbiting around him.
'*Moh*' has the strength of gravity's pull.

समय

नई आदत लगी है मिट्टी खाने की
बताओ तो . . .
ज़मीं का स्वाद कैसा है?
ज़मीं पूरी की पूरी पेश कर सकता हूँ तुमको,
मगर सब चाट जाओगे,
तो रहने के लिये कैसे बचेगी?

मेरी मानो . . . इसे छोड़ो
किसी दिन आसमाँ चाटेंगे, चलकर
सुना है, आम पापड़ की तरह 'खटा मिट्ठा' होता है!

Samay

Your new habit of eating soil
Tell me, how does the ground taste
I can present you with the whole earth
But if you lick it all up
What will remain to live on?

Listen to me, let this be
Someday, let us go and lick the sky
I'm told like aam-papad, it's a little bit sweet
And a little bit sour.

समय

जन्म दिन था तीसरा और
नानी, दादी, दोनों तुतला कर
एक कहानी सुना रही थीं
दोनों के मुँह टेढ़े मेढ़े होने लगे थे
मैं देख रहा था
बहला बहला कर कोशिश में थीं कि तुम सो जाओ
लेकिन तुम हैरानी से उनके मुँह देख रहे थे
बोले 'नाना
आपस में तो ठीक से बातें कर लेती हैं
मेरे सामने आते ही क्यों दोनों तुतलाने लगती हैं?'

Samay

Your third birthday, and
both your grannies, Nani and Dadi
Were lisping out stories.
Both of them making funny, crooked faces
I was watching . . .

Cajoling you, trying in various ways,
To make you fall asleep
But you were watching their faces in amazement.
You said, 'Nana,
By themselves they speak perfectly well
But why, when they face me, do they start to lisp?'

समय

नानी के फ़ार्म, फ़ार्म नहीं देहात कहो तुम
फ़ार्म पे जाकर तुम पूरे देहाती लगते हो !

बन्यान, कच्छा, पहन के हौज़ में पत्थर फेंकने लगते हो
और हर बार 'गुड़प' मुँह से आवाज़ भी करते हो
मिट्टी, ग़ारा, कुट्टी, चारा, सब करना होता है
आवाज़ लगाते हो 'धन्नो' गैया को बुलाते हो
'धन्नो' गोबर करे तो जाकर चुग़ली करते हो

'नानी, नानी, देखो धन्नो, पॉटी करती है !'

Samay

Your nani's farm, actually
You should call it a village
You look a typical rustic when you visit it.
Wearing *banian* and *kachha* you start throwing stones in the pond
Making a 'gudup' sound with each throw
Mud, slurry, chaff, fodder, you participate in all.

You call out to the cow, Dhannu, in your voice
And run to tattle about her making *gobar*
'Nani Nani, look Dhannu is doing potty.'

पाली

मेरा बोकसर! उसे कुत्ता कभी नहीं कहा मैंने!

पाली

किसी तारीक कोने में छुपी थी
ताक में बैठी हुई थी
ज़रा बीमार था, कमज़ोर था पाली
झपटा मार के बस ले गयी उसको!

ये सब खाती है . . .
कोई ज़ात है इस मौत की
न धरम है कोई!

Pali

My Boxer. I never called him a dog.

Pali

One day, hidden in a corner
Of the ledge, She was sitting.
Pali was a bit weak, somewhat sick
She snapped him up, and took him away.

She eats everything . . .
Death has no caste
Or code of conduct.

Scan QR code to access the
Penguin Random House India website